author's note

Dear Reader,

Sad Perfect is an extremely personal novel that I wrote while my daughter was in an outpatient program for her diagnosis of ARFID (Avoidant/Restrictive Food Intake Disorder)—a serious eating disorder that is often described as a form of extremely picky eating, but is becoming better understood as a fear of food with both psychological and physical components.

If you are easily triggered about eating disorders, hospitalization, suicidal ideation, self-harm, or drug use and abuse, please reconsider reading *Sad Perfect*.

While I did my best to present accurate information about ARFID, *Sad Perfect* is a work of fiction. Pea is a fictional character created to represent what I hope is an authentic account of what it's like to live with ARFID and how one family experienced it. This book is not intended to serve as a diagnostic tool nor as a substitute for the expertise of qualified mental health professionals.

No two stories are alike. You may be struggling. If you are, please know that help is available. This is a story written to show how one family found healing and recovery in the hopes that it would inspire others to do the same.

Most sincerely,
Stephanie Elliot

Do you need help?

National Eating Disorders Association
Website: https://www.nationaleatingdisorders.org
Phone: 1-800-931-2237

National Suicide Prevention Hotline:
Website: https://suicidepreventionlifeline.org
Phone: 1-800-273-8255

National Alliance on Mental Illness:
Website: https://www.nami.org/Learn-More/Mental-Health-Conditions/Related-Conditions/Self-harm
Phone: 1-800-950-NAMI

sad perfect

Stephanie Elliot

SQUARE
FISH

Margaret Ferguson Books
FARRAR STRAUS GIROUX
New York

SQUARE
FISH

An imprint of Macmillan Publishing Group, LLC
175 Fifth Avenue, New York, NY 10010
fiercereads.com

Square Fish and the Square Fish logo are trademarks of Macmillan and
are used by Farrar Straus Giroux under license from Macmillan.

Our books may be purchased in bulk for promotional, educational, or business
use. Please contact your local bookseller or the Macmillan Corporate and
Premium Sales Department at (800) 221-7945 ext. 5442 or by e-mail at
MacmillanSpecialMarkets@macmillan.com.

Library of Congress Cataloging-in-Publication Data

Names: Elliot, Stephanie, author.
Title: Sad perfect / Stephanie Elliot.
Description: New York : Farrar Straus Giroux, 2017. | "Margaret Ferguson books." |
    Summary: "The story of a teen girl's struggle with Avoidant/Restrictive Food
    Intake Disorder and how love helps her on the road to recovery"–Provided by
    publisher.
Identifiers: LCCN 2016013348 (print) | LCCN 2016037176 (ebook) |
    ISBN 978-1-250-14417-1 (paperback)   ISBN 978-0-374-30377-8 (ebook)
Subjects: | CYAC: Eating disorders–Fiction. | Love–Fiction. | BISAC: JUVENILE
    FICTION / Social Issues / Depression & Mental Illness. | JUVENILE FICTION /
    Social Issues / Dating & Sex.
Classification: LCC PZ7.1.E443 Sad 2017 (print) | LCC PZ7.1.E443 (ebook) |
    DDC [Fic]–dc23
LC record available at https://lccn.loc.gov/2016013348

Originally published in the United States by Farrar Straus Giroux
First Square Fish edition, 2018
Book designed by Andrew Arnold
Square Fish logo designed by Filomena Tuosto

1   3   5   7   9   10   8   6   4   2

To my daughter, McKaelen.
You know for every reason why. 1–4–3

sad perfect

You float.

It's hot out, not kind of hot, not medium hot, but midsummer-Arizona hot. Sweltering one hundred and twelve degrees, and you're floating on the Salt River, the first time ever, on one of those black inner tubes, the old-fashioned, tar-smelling ones that need to be inflated with a tire pump. You've already scratched your upper thigh on that poky thing where the air goes in, because you thought it would be easier to put the tube around your waist to lug it into the mucky river. It slid down your body and scraped your leg, leaving a big red welt.

This was not your idea of tubing.

Your idea of tubing was hanging on to a rope from the back of a speedboat while the cool wind whipped through your hair. You imagined clinging to a tube specially designed for the activity, and you would be on a lake, not a crappy river filled with snakes and fish and mud and slimy plants that would wrap around your ankles if you dared to stand for a second and let your feet sink into the gooey bottom.

But it's your best friend Jae's sixteenth birthday and her mom planned this surprise for her, and so you came along, not expecting anything like this. There are mostly family members and some friends from her soccer team and church group. Now you're scorching in the sun, trying to stay cool, wishing more than anything that you could somehow fast-forward this "tubing" experience, because it's an expected four-hour "float" down the Salt River on burning-hot black inner tubes, and most of the party has gained momentum and you're stuck in the back with a few stragglers you don't know.

So you float. And you're miserable. And you're stuck.

You plop your hand into the water and splash some droplets onto your chest, trying to cool off. Your mom didn't want you to wear the bathing suit you wanted to wear because in her opinion it's too revealing, so you lied to her and told her you wouldn't. Then you brought the one you wanted to wear and changed into it anyway. Because what does your mother know? She doesn't remember what it was like to be sixteen. She doesn't understand the things you need to be concerned with, like wearing a good bathing suit in a crappy river.

But right now, the only thing you have to do is float.

So there's a lot of time for you to think.

You're really good at thinking, and there's a lot to think about. Like about how you look, and how you wish you looked different. You're too tall. You wish your nose wasn't so slopey. You hate that your eyebrows could be waxed every week, but your mom only lets you get them waxed every month. You hate the girls your own age, except for Jae. They're mostly high-pitched girls who only care about how many Instagram likes they have or how many Twitter retweets they get and you wonder what makes them so popular. Most days you wonder what it would be like if the universe were different.

You wonder, if you feel this way on a partially good day–because you know this is supposed to be a good day–how you are going to feel when a bad day hits. Because you also know a bad day is bound to come soon. It's been a while. There's been a slew of not-so-bad days, and on this partially good day, when the sun is shining, and you're floating, you should be feeling good, right?

"You're having fun, aren't you?" Jae asks when you stop at the midway point for lunch.

"Sure," you say, nodding. "It's fun."

You touch her chest and the spot flames from white to bright red under your fingertip. "You're getting sunburned."

"So're you," Jae says, poking you back.

So you slather each other up with some more sunscreen, which you know isn't going to do jack shit to keep you from burning because you're pretty fair anyway, but it's better than nothing.

Jae's mom sets food on a rickety wooden picnic table. Lucky

her, she opted out of the river ride and delivered lunch instead, although eating lunch is not exactly your favorite activity either. You stand awkwardly while everyone fills their paper plates with hot dogs, chips, potato salad, and fruit. Jae's mom catches your eye. "Lunchtime?"

You're doing this little back-and-forth on your heels, feeling jittery, and you pick at your fingernails. "My mom made pancakes for breakfast. I'm not hungry." One of those statements is true, but you aren't going to eat with the group. You can't. "I'll have a Coke though?"

"Sure, over there." She points to the blue-and-white cooler past the picnic table.

A guy from the party is by the cooler. You saw him earlier, noticed he was really cute, wanted to get a better look at him, maybe ask Jae who he was, but then he had disappeared into the river with everyone else. Now though, he's right in front of you. Shirtless. Smiling.

"Hey," he says.

"Hi," you say.

"You friends with Jae?"

"Yep."

"Me too. Well, I'm her cousin's friend. I never met her before. Braden asked her if I could come."

"It's too hot," you say. Then you want to kick yourself because you're being negative.

But he agrees with you. "Way too hot. You want a drink?"

"Yeah, please."

He bends down and plunges his hand into the icy water to search for a can, and you get a better look at him. You already noticed he is taller than you, a lot taller, probably six inches taller. He's got thick, dark hair, and his back is muscular and tan. When he stands up to give you your drink he sees you staring at him and he half grins.

"This one okay?" he asks as he hands you a root beer.

"Yeah, it's good." You laugh.

2

Lunch is over, well, for those who ate, and now everyone is being corralled back into the murky water. This is the part you've been warned about, where it might get a little bit fast on the river, with some small rapids, and Jae's mom says to be careful.

"Make sure not to lag so far behind this time," Jae yells to you as you lug the tube to the river. The black tire burns your hands and you drop it to the ground. You can't believe how stupid hot it is out. You set your sunglasses over your eyes and grab your hair and try to create a makeshift bun, but it's impossible without a hair tie. You let your hair fall down over your shoulders. You swat at a fly buzzing in your face.

"You better get in, or you're going to lose everyone."

It's the boy. He's standing behind you, waiting.

It's silly really to call him a boy. He's not a boy, he's more like a . . . Well, you don't know what he is, except perfect. And this time you look at all of him, and you can't think of a thing to say.

"Go on, slowpoke." He nudges your tube with his tube. "Need help?"

Everyone is already in the water, laughing and waiting.

"Sure. Yeah." You barely manage the words.

He lifts your tube easily, his muscles hardly straining at holding two of them, and you see he's got those awesome veins running through his forearms. You wonder if this is really happening.

He strides ahead of you a few steps.

"Come on." He nods in the direction of the water.

You follow quickly because this is really happening . . . and *arm veins*!

He flips the tubes into the water effortlessly. You try as delicately as you can to arrange yourself onto your tube. Then you're off. Floating.

You and the perfect boy.

Suddenly, it's the most beautiful day. You're not in the rapids yet and the river is calm. The sky is translucent and there's not a cloud anywhere. Just blue, blue, blue. And a spot of sun.

If you look at the sun for too long, you know it'll hurt, but it's one of those suns that burns bright, it's one of those suns that begs to be stared into. You can't help yourself. And when you close your eyes everything flashes white except that spot where the sun was—it's turned black, blinding.

You're sprawled out on your back on the tube, knees bent, ankles and feet plunged into the water, your fingertips skimming the glassy top layer of the river. You're floating, just floating, thinking of endless possibilities, when the boy says, so near to you that you practically jump, "Do you have a name?"

You tell him your name and he says he's never heard that before and you tell him you get that a lot.

He says it's pretty.

You feel yourself blush but then you're not sure if it's the sun on your face or if you're really feeling a little blushy. You turn your face to get a better look at him.

"What's your name?" you ask him.

"Ben."

"Hi, Ben."

He moves his tube closer to yours and grabs on to it so he's right next to you. You tense up a bit, but then remind yourself to relax. That this is a not-so-bad day, a partially good day actually, and you're wearing your favorite bathing suit. It's just you and Ben; and Jae and all her friends and family floating up ahead.

You're close enough to notice his brown eyes—dark as Hershey's chocolate Kisses—and he's smiling at you, so you don't look away. He asks if you're still hot and you say a little, and then you worry he's one of those jerky guys who might try to flip you over on the tube, and maybe try to make your top fall off, but instead he just dips his hand into the river and drips some water onto your shoulders to cool you off. Which feels really nice and you think it was a sweet thing for him to do.

"Thanks." You smile at him. It's the smile you've practiced in the mirror. The smile-at-boys smile. You hope it turned out right.

He asks where you go to school and you tell him. When you say you are going to be a junior, he says he thought maybe you were a senior. He's going to be a junior too, although he's almost seventeen and you turned sixteen in May, so you're about a year apart in age. He goes to one of the other high schools in town and you don't know any of the same people. He runs track and used to play football but didn't like it. "The guys are all douche bags."

You mention that your brother plays football.

"Not all football players are douche bags," Ben says, smiling.

"Oh no, they totally are, my brother included," you say, and laugh.

He asks if you play any sports and you say no but you like to draw. He asks you to tell him more about it so you explain you mostly sketch, and you like to do line drawings and create cartoon figures.

"I took a ceramics class last year but I got a C," he says. "I sucked at it."

"I had a tough time in my ceramics class," you say, because you want to be sympathetic, and also because it *was* hard. "Throwing clay on the wheel was the worst."

11

You're floating closer to the rapids and you're getting jostled in your tube; water splashes everywhere.

"It looks a little rough ahead," Ben says, and grasps your tube a bit tighter.

"This part scares me," you admit.

"Don't worry, I'll make sure you're safe," he says.

Jae's ahead of you and she and some of her friends laugh loudly and a couple of the girls mock-scream. She sees you and waves and you wave back.

There are small whitecaps of rapids and the quiet calm of the river has changed to a whooshing rush of water. The river has also gotten deeper. Your heart speeds up and you close your eyes and tense your body as you and Ben start careening through the rapids.

For a moment or two, things seem okay, but then there's an unexpected drop in the river, not too deep, but enough that Ben loses his grip on your tube. The good news is, once you've hit that drop, you're coming out of the rapids. The bad news is, you've fallen out of your tube.

Just before you're about to go under, you feel arms reach around your waist and Ben, no longer in his tube, pulls you up in to him.

You thought you were going to lose your breath before, but when you're this close to him, and he's holding you like this, you really can't breathe. He's got your tube, and he's holding you in the water, looking right into your eyes. He asks, "Can you get back on?"

"I think so."

Ben lets go of you to steady your tube. Instead of climbing on top, you plunge under the water and swim up through the hole. You wrap your arms over the top of the tube and hold on, so your arms are hanging over the sides and your legs are submerged deep within the hole of the tube.

"Okay, I'll go grab mine," he says.

He swims to his tube, disappears under, and gets in just like you did. When he comes back, he reaches out and you grab his hand and pull him to your tube.

"Thanks," he says. You are now face-to-face, both of you in the middle of your tubes, arms hanging over the sides. There are those arm veins again.

You expect him to let go of your hand, to just hold on to your tube, but he doesn't. Instead, he takes your other hand too, and rearranges his fingers so they are intertwined with yours. He moves his thumb over your knuckle, and his eyes light up, as bright as the sun on this beautiful, strange day.

"That was kinda crazy," he says.

"Yeah."

The water caresses your skin, the sun is a blanket of warmth on your back, and Ben slides his thumb over and over the top of your hand, like he's been around forever, like you haven't known him for only a couple of hours.

You feel it, you feel everything, all the way through to your toes.

You both stay like that, talking, looking into the too-bright sunshine, and into each other's eyes, holding hands for the rest of the afternoon.

It's more than a not-so-bad, partially good day.

You're holding hands.

You're floating.

3

You're in your room, listening to music, and there's that knock.
Your parents have asked you not to lock your door, so you don't
lock it and they have mostly respected your privacy by knock-
ing. You want to lock your bedroom door though, because
it's your room, it's the only place you feel like yourself, and it's
not like you're doing anything bad. You're just lying here.
Thinking.

You think about how you need to take that little yellow pill
every day to be in a sort of good mood, and it generally doesn't
even guarantee you'll be in a good mood.

You wonder if you're going to have to take that pill every
day for the rest of your life.

You think about how often people comment on how tall and
beautiful you are, and how you wish you could believe them.
Why can't you believe them?

You think about how freaked out you are about school starting next month.

You think about what picture you'll put on Instagram next, and if your mom will yell at you for exposing too much cleavage. (*I didn't have boobs like* that *when I was your age!* she'll say. You'll remind her they didn't have social media or iPhones *or the Internet* when she was sixteen and she rode to school on a dinosaur. You do love your mom, you do.)

You think about how your lips are always chapped and you should get some new lip gloss.

You think about Alex but then you make yourself not think about Alex.

You think about how you're a little bit hungry. Then decide you're not.

You think about how you held hands with Ben just yesterday and how it was practically one of the most perfect days you've had in a very long time.

You're thinking about the sunburn you got and wishing you had put more sunscreen on—damn your mother for always being right about the stupid sunscreen.

You're also thinking about how it is worth a thousand sunburns to have had the day you had.

You think about how awful it is to be lonely, and you're tired of feeling this way.

You think about the girl from school who has two hundred thousand followers on Instagram and wonder how she got so many followers; what is it that makes her so popular?

You think about becoming an artist someday. Even though

you know that a job in the arts would not make much money, you feel that being an artist would make you happy.

Your mind never shuts off and it gets terribly exhausting.

There's that knock again.

"Can I come in, please?" your mom asks.

Your mom is usually the one looking for you. Your older brother, Todd, hardly bothers with you. Your dad, when he's not at work, is mostly always watching ESPN.

"Sure."

You turn off your music and wait.

Your mom comes in; she's holding a glass of wine and has that sweet-sickening smile, the one that's all cheery and upbeat.

"Dinner's ready." She takes a sip of wine and that happy-fake smirk makes you want to bury your head in your pillow and scream.

"I'm not hungry."

She already knows that. You know she knows that. This is the game you both play. It's been going on for years, pretty much your whole life, yet you still play it.

"Can't you come down and sit with us? You can eat what-ever you want."

Another sip of wine.

"I don't feel like it."

You open your laptop. Like the discussion is over. Like you can control the situation.

"Not even an apple?"

"Mom."

"Fine. But I have some news for you. That place I've mentioned before, Healthy Foundations? They called me back, and you have an appointment this Thursday. Your dad and I want you to go."

You don't look at her. Because you know. Deep in your heart, you know. You've been waiting for this and it's almost a relief to hear that she's going to take care of the problem: ever since you were a little girl, ever since you have had a memory, you haven't liked food, except for the obvious good stuff–the safe foods.

The healthy foods that have protein and vitamins–the vital nutritious food–you don't eat. It's pretty much impossible. You've never known why–and it's not that you haven't tried, because you have tried, many times–but you have no desire to eat those things. Ever. You wish so much that you could enjoy food the way others do. But you can't because something is there, stuck in your throat–a monster, guarding its castle, your body, and it won't let the stuff go down. The monster comes and goes sporadically, but when you're feeling stressed or anxious about food you know it's his doing. You know it seems silly, but that's the only way to explain it, yet you've never been able to tell a doctor this. Because it sounds so stupid, that a monster lives inside you.

And you know your problem is not anorexia or bulimia, because you've never wanted to lose weight, and you've never thrown up, hidden food, used laxatives, or binged. The only time you've purposely not eaten was when that thing with Alex happened last spring and that doesn't count.

When you do eat the foods you can eat—your safe foods—the monster is usually quiet. You don't limit your portions, you don't worry about how much you put into your mouth, you don't think about gagging. You've always had a healthy-looking body, and that's one of the reasons your parents could keep denying something was wrong. You're neither too thin nor too heavy. Throughout your whole life, no matter where your parents have taken you to be evaluated—the pediatrician or a nutritionist—they always came to the same conclusion—that you're a healthy, normal girl who is simply a "picky" eater.

You're perfect.

But there's more.

Because the monster also makes it extremely hard for you to do things a normal girl is able to do. The monster was lingering at Jae's party, making it hard to socialize, making it impossible to eat with friends. He causes anxiety and depression, and makes you sad because he's holding you back from so many things you'd like to do, from so many things you know you *want* to do but are incapable of doing.

So when your mom tells you she's made an appointment, you feel that maybe the monster took a hit. At least maybe he got stabbed or something. Like the battle has begun.

"You're good with this?" your mom asks.

You look up from your laptop and shrug. You have all sorts of feelings but aren't sure how to react. You're scared and anxious, and you don't know what's coming your way or what you'll have to do to get the monster to die.

You just know you want the monster out of you. He's lived there far too long.

4

"Braden said Ben wants your phone number."

It is the next night and you and Jae are on FaceTime, and when she says this, you tilt your head down and pick at your blue toenail polish so she can't see that your face lights up. Even though your room is dark because you've got candles lit and there are flickering shadows everywhere. The candles soothe you and they smell good, but your mom gets annoyed when you light them. ("You're going to burn down the house one of these days," she's always saying.)

"Did you give it to him? My number?" you ask.

"No! I wasn't going to give out your number to just anyone."

"Well, you can give it to him."

"Uh, well, what exactly is going on?" Jae moves her face closer to the screen, scrutinizing you through the Mac.

Your smile goes big. You try to pull it back in but it's no use.

"What happened on the river?" she asks.

Jae knows everything about you. She knows about the

monster. She helps feed it when it's hungry. She calms you when the monster makes you anxious and she cheers you up when the monster makes you depressed. Jae probably wants it dead just as much as you do. She's been your best—really, only—friend since you met each other in first grade. She doesn't judge you. She understands you. You tell her everything. She's the closest person in your life, next to your mom, who sometimes drives you crazy.

But Jae, Jae means the world to you. She's nothing like the girls at school who live and breathe by how many likes they get on Instagram; Jae doesn't care what others think about her. You wish you could be more like her. Jae has that balance between caring and not caring too much. You need to find that balance. You want to be like her but you're not jealous of her. You just love her.

So you tell her about Ben. How he made you smile, how he cooled you off when you got too hot, how he helped you when the rapids got rough, how his lips curled up at the edges when you said something funny. How he made you feel like you were funny. How he said he liked tall girls. How he held your hands and you felt it all the way to your toes, a tingling that you've never felt with any boy.

"Not even when you first dated Alex?" Jae's eyes go wide on the screen.

"Ugh, I can't believe I wasted my time with Alex. Oh my God, Jae. When Ben and I held hands, I can't even..." When you think about it now, you still feel the warmth that flooded your body. You want to feel it again.

"Text Braden my number right now!" you say.

"I'm texting him!"

You watch the computer screen as she texts your number. "Oh my God, I'm so excited for you!" Jae says. She's the *best* best friend.

"Okay, he texted me back. He's going to text it to Ben!"

You kneel on your bed and emit a little girlie squeal and then want to shove it back into your mouth, because you sound like one of those stupid girls. You don't want to be a stupid girl.

Suddenly, you're starving. You grab your Mac and Jae and take them into the kitchen. Todd's on the couch with his earbuds in and he's furiously texting someone. Dad's probably still at work. Your mom is doing dishes from dinner, which you skipped.

"Hi, what's up?" she asks.

"Nothing," you say.

"Hi Mrs. Richards," Jae says from your laptop screen.

"Hi Jae," your mom says, and moves in front of your Mac to give Jae a quick wave.

You look in the fridge and you don't know why because you never like anything in there. Maybe sometimes an apple. You open the pantry and grab the Ritz crackers.

"Why don't you put some peanut butter on those," your mom suggests.

"Mom."

Your mom holds her hands up in protest.

You actually like peanut butter but you're not in the mood for it.

"It's just, I think you should probably have some protein," your mom says.

"I'll get a Carnation Instant milk."

You make your milk and take it and the crackers up to your room, along with Jae and your Mac.

"No crumbs!" your mom yells from the kitchen.

"Fine!"

In your room you settle onto your bed, not caring if you get crumbs all over.

"So," you say to Jae, "guess where Mom's taking me this week."

"I don't know, where?"

"One of those places."

"What places?"

You roll your eyes at the screen and move your face close to where Jae can see you very clearly.

"You know," you say, "one of those eating-disorder places."

It's the first time you've ever said the words aloud.

Hey?

Hey

It's Ben. From the river.

I know. Hi.☺

Hey. You still sunburned?

LOL. Of course! It's only been 3 days! I hurt!

Me too, I got burned bad

Yeah

So, it's OK I got your number?

Of course

Good

So . . .

Um . . .

LOL . . .

So did you have fun?

It definitely got better

That's for sure

. . .

Do you wanna go see a movie tomorrow night?

Sure

You haven't been on a real date before, where the guy picks you up in his car. You and Alex were only sophomores, and dating consisted of going out in a small group of friends to the mall or movies, so this is for-real real. And you're nervous. So nervous that you haven't eaten all day long, when normally you might have had at least a couple of waffles for breakfast. Your mom makes you drink some milk and eat a few crackers at four o'clock. She asks if you remembered to take your pill that morning. You nod yes in between dry, pasty cracker bites. You never forget it. You know that's the difference between having a crap day and a maybe non-crap day.

Your mom watches as you take small bites of your crackers and drink your milk. She says, "I hope you have fun tonight," but you can tell she doesn't really mean what she says, and for some reason, you think she doesn't want you going out. Your dad is watching a preseason football game. You have no idea where Todd is, and you actually care. You might miss the idea of your family. You feel like it's maybe falling apart. Maybe it's the monster's fault. Could that monster that lingers in the crevices of your brain have that much power over so many people? He's pretty powerful. But you push the feelings aside, because you want this to be a not-so-bad night, you want this to be a good night. No, scratch that. You want this to be a phenomenal night.

Jae comes over and helps you pick out an outfit, one that's not too datey looking, not too casual, one that says, *I'm confident, and I look nice, and I'm not easy, and I like you.* It's difficult to come up with the right combination. You decide on white jeans with a black tank and a pair of strappy black sandals. Then you add a pink-and-black scarf in case it gets cold in the theater, also for a pop of color.

Jae hugs you goodbye and tells you to text her later, then you go to the living room to peek out the front window and wait for Ben. At five minutes before six, a silver SUV pulls up and Ben gets out. He rakes his fingers through his hair like he's nervous and that makes you like him even more and you relax for a split second.

He wears belted khaki shorts and a white V-neck T-shirt and Vans and you think you might die a little bit inside at how handsome he is. You hadn't seen him like this before—dressed. Although he had looked incredible wearing just his Hurley board shorts when you met at the river.

He rings the bell and you wait a beat before answering the door. Your smile goes wide when you see him.

"Hi," you say, hanging back a bit behind the half-opened door.

"Hi," he says, grinning wildly at you.

"Come on in." You open the door the rest of the way to let him in as your parents come to the foyer.

"Mom, Dad, this is Ben. He's Jae's cousin's friend. We met Saturday at Jae's party."

"Hi Ben, nice to meet you," your mom says. You can tell she thinks he's cute and then you think that maybe she's okay with this after all.

Your dad shakes his hand and immediately goes into sports talk, because that's what dads do.

"Hi Ben, you play basketball?" Your dad asks this because Ben's like six-four.

"No sir. I used to play football, but now I run track," he replies.

"Oh cool. I bet you're great at the long jump." Your dad sounds stupid and you roll your eyes at Ben.

Todd walks past with his earbuds in and gives a wave and says, "What's up."

Ben says, "Hey," and nods. It seems to be a universal guy thing, and you don't care to introduce Todd to Ben so it's fine when your brother takes two steps at a time up the stairs and disappears into the black hole that is his room.

"You two going to see a movie?" your mom asks.

"Yes, and then maybe something to eat after, if that's okay?" Ben asks.

"Sure," your dad says, then looks at you. "You know the rules, Pea." And he actually winks at you, which pretty much mortifies you and you go into daughter mode and say, "Daddy!" and everyone laughs and you say, "We're going now, bye!"

Of course it's then that your dad decides to take ownership over you and gives you a big hug and a kiss and says, "Be good."

You grab your purse and your phone, kiss your mom, and say, "I will," and, "Bye."

Ben says, "It's nice to meet you," and your parents say it to him too. They sound sincere, and it makes you happy to think he's made a good impression on them, because you don't want your parents to not like him.

When you're finally out of your house, you say, "Oh God, I'm sorry about that."

"Hey, they were fine," Ben says, laughing.

"They're probably spying from the front window right now."

"You think so? They seem nice," Ben says.

"I guess."

"Your dad calls you Pea?"

"You caught that?" you ask.

"Yeah. It's a cute nickname. How'd you get it?"

You smirk. "Long story."

"Hmm," he says.

He walks you to the passenger door and opens it for you and you squeal a little inside because this is the first time a guy has ever opened a car door for you and it's just too much. You catch a whiff of Ben's cologne and you think, *Oh my God*, because he smells like Abercrombie & Fitch, but not like how when you walk into the store and get a massive headache, just how if you walk *by* the store and get a quick whiff of it. A mix of that and soap. Yes, that's what you think he smells like. Like a little bit of Abercrombie & Fitch, not too much, and good soap. Perfect.

He waits for you to get into the car and then he leans in and you can smell him even more. He says, "Well, nickname or not, you look very pretty."

He shuts the door and you absolutely want to die.

7

On the way to the movies, Ben plays music from one of your favorite bands, and then some stuff you've never heard by some indie guy from Ireland who he said you might like and you do. His car is extremely neat and you're pretty sure he vacuumed it out especially for you, and these little facts make you feel like you could really, really like Ben–more than you think you already do. You notice that he's got his hands set on the steering wheel at ten and two, just like you learned in Drivers Ed, and you get a bit giddy thinking he's a cautious driver, and also, you check out his arm veins again, and that makes you even more giddy. Then you remember how he held your hands as you floated down the Salt River and you get all warm and tingly inside thinking maybe he'll hold your hand in the theater.

You don't know how you're going to survive this date. You're not even there yet and it already seems too fantastic.

The movie you planned on seeing, a thriller about spies in Italy, is sold out, so you agree to see a different one, a better one, in your opinion, one that you would have chosen, about a quirky college kid trying to beat the system.

Before you go find seats Ben asks if you want some popcorn or candy and you say no.

"Maybe a drink though?" you suggest.

"Wanna share one? They're pretty big," he says. You both agree on a Sprite. With two straws.

In the theater, when he leads you to almost the back row, your palms start to sweat and you wonder if he's that type of guy. Then he asks, "Is this okay? I hate sitting up close because it kills my neck since I'm so tall."

It makes sense to you, so you say sure.

When you sit, at first you don't know what to do with your hands, so you keep them in your lap.

You're with this great guy, and this is pretty much officially your first real date, because even though you and Alex were "dating" for four months, you never really went out on dates, and in the end he was a total jerk. You make yourself stop thinking about Alex, try to focus on what's happening now. You inhale deeply, and when you do, you smell Ben, and he smells like you already want to commit him to memory.

You're trying to make sense of the whole experience, and it hasn't even happened yet. But you're sure it's happening.

"You okay?" he asks.

You decide to try honesty.

"This is kind of a first for me," you say.

"First PG-13 movie?"

This makes you laugh and you're grateful. He's got the best smile, and such beautiful straight white teeth, and you're comfortable enough with him that you give his arm a quick nudge. Plus, you want to touch him.

"I'm a little bit nervous."

"You don't have to be. I like you. And it's just a movie. Look, those guys don't seem nervous at all." Ben points to a couple a few rows ahead of you who are making out and you giggle.

"Think it's *their* first date?" you ask.

"Doubt it." He grins and takes a sip of the Sprite.

The theater goes dark and the previews start. People silence their phones and turn their screen lights to Low. You turn your phone to Vibrate; you're sure no one is going to call you, although Jae might text, and then you see Ben turn his phone completely off. He holds the Sprite out for you. "Want a sip?"

"Sure."

Halfway through the movie you have to pee. Really bad. There's no holding it.

"I have to pee," you whisper to Ben.

He laughs. "Don't do it here."

You stand and when you pass him, he touches your leg. "Hurry back," he says.

When you return, you're fully aware that he's moved the soda to his right and lifted the armrest that separated the two of you. You're nervous and also a little bit excited.

"Did I miss anything good?"

"Nah. He just threw a kegger at the frat he started."

You sit down and what happens next is perfect. Ben moves closer to you, takes your hand in his, and places his other hand over it. "You doing okay?" he whispers into your ear.

"Yeah," you whisper. "I'm really good."

And you mean it.

He makes you good.

"Good."

You tune out the movie. There is no more guy running a frat house. It's just Ben holding your hand, rubbing slow circles on your palm with his thumb and it's crazy amazing. You rest your head on his shoulder. It feels like you've known him forever. He feels like comfort. He relaxes you. His hand is large and warm and protective. It's not sweaty and awkward like it was with Alex. It feels natural, like his hand was meant to hold yours—two parts of a puzzle that fit.

Ben says, "I'm not letting go. I'm just going to hold your hand till the movie's over."

You sigh.

8

You and your mom have different perspectives on what you used to like to eat as a kid. Of course, you don't remember what you ate as a two-year-old, but she insists you liked regular kid foods. She says you ate bananas and hot dogs, hamburgers and jelly sandwiches cut into tiny squares, and macaroni and cheese, and spaghetti with red sauce. She says you ate blueberries and cantaloupe for a while, and that you used to ask for more. More blueberries until the outside of your lips turned purplish-red and she had to take the container away from you. But you don't remember any of that. You're sure she's confusing you with Todd.

What *you* remember is that you never liked food, only that sometimes you craved salt and sometimes you craved sugar and when that happened you needed to have something salty or sweet right away, and you'd get cranky if you didn't. Your mom says you were a "challenging" baby, a "precocious" toddler; that's how she describes you to Shayna, the therapist at Healthy Foundations.

"She's always just been stubborn," your mom tells Shayna.

Shayna nods, jots down a note, then says, "We like to use the phrase 'strong-willed.' Our girls are strong-willed." And she smiles. You like this about her. That she turned a negative word into a positive, so you sit up a bit straighter and try to tune in. Because before you heard the phrase "strong-willed" you were hearing a lot of "blah-blah-blueberries-blah" coming out of your mom's mouth, and it was annoying.

"Yes, she's very strong-willed," your mother agrees with Shayna. "She does what she wants to do. And we've never been the type of parents who forced her to eat. I wasn't going to do that to her. I wasn't going to leave her at the table all night with a piece of meat she didn't want to eat and wait it out. I couldn't do that."

You look at your mom because her voice cracks and you're afraid she might cry and more than almost anything in the world, you hate seeing your mom cry.

Shayna writes something else down, then turns her attention to you. You like the way she's dressed, sharp and stylish, nice pants and a shirt with fancy buttons, like she might have shopped in the Juniors section. And her jewelry's on point. She's also got these funky glasses that she probably needs to see stuff up close, but they don't make her look old, they just make her look more like a hipster. You think your mom should probably get some style tips from her while you're getting eating tips. You laugh a little inside when you think about this. A two-for-one– help dress your mom, help you eat.

"So," Shayna says, and looks at you. "What about you?" She smiles kindly.

You half shrug and suddenly you're really nervous, like you're being called out. You feel your blood go cold. You're not sure what to say. Because the monster has taken over. He's taken over your voice and you can't talk for a few seconds. But you shove the monster back down and find your voice. Because you know you've got to be stronger than the monster that has controlled your life for practically sixteen years if you're going to get better.

You speak.

"I wish I liked food. But I don't."

Shayna jots it down, you're sure, word for word.

"Stuff just doesn't taste good to me. I can't put food into my mouth. It's just, it's just . . . gross." There's no other way for you to describe it. Food in your mouth is not pleasing. You eat to survive, and only to survive, barely. Sometimes you see something, like cake or ice cream, and that's different. That, you want. That, you know is comforting. That, you know is safe. You tell this to Shayna, and she writes it down.

You keep talking. Sixteen years of built-up silence spills out: how you feel like you're letting your family down, how you feel like you're to blame for your parents arguing about you not eating, how you feel like your family doesn't even feel like a family because you mostly don't eat with them, how your brother doesn't even acknowledge you anymore, how he couldn't care less if you existed. And the tears come and you heave and cry and you watch as your mom cries too, and it's painful and sad and all you want, more than anything in the world, is to get better, and to be able to eat a regular meal and have it not feel like you're chewing human flesh and like it's killing you. You say this out loud to Shayna too. And your mom brings her hand to her mouth in shock.

"Mom, stop. Don't cry," you say. This is your pain. Your trauma, and you have to console your goddamn mother. What the fuck.

Shayna hands you a box of tissues and then goes back to her writing. You think she writes too much. Then she asks, "What do you eat? What is your favorite thing to eat?"

You take a deep breath before answering her.

"Bread."

"What else?" Shayna asks.

"French fries, with ketchup," you say. "Waffles, pancakes."

"No syrup or butter," your mom interjects.

You glare at your mother.

"Go on." Shayna addresses you.

"Pizza."

Your mom says, "She takes the cheese off."

You give your mom another death stare. "Do *you* want to tell her, *Mom*?"

So your mom does. "She eats apples sometimes, and carrots, and white foods, but not pasta or rice or potatoes. Nothing like that. She does eat peanut butter, thank God, for the limited protein. Bagels. She eats cake and muffins, but no muffins that have nuts or fruit. Only muffins that have chocolate chips. She loves chocolate. And ice cream. And crackers. Goldfish and Ritz and saltines. Basically all plain crackers. Sometimes she'll eat cereal. Potato chips, pretzels, that kind of stuff. And pop. No orange juice. Oh, she loves apple juice, but no other type of juice. She drinks milk, and occasionally she'll have a yogurt, thank God, thank God for that..."

Your mother drones on and on about you and your eating habits. If you were five years old, you'd clamp your hands over your ears and scream really loud. Instead you sit silently, letting the tears streak down your cheeks. They just fall and fall and fall and you've never hated your mother more.

You've also never loved her so much.

9

"Hey Pea."

Your dad has called you Pea since before you existed. That's what they tell you. That your parents found out they were pregnant and they were thrilled. But then a week later, your mom started bleeding and they thought they were losing you. The ultrasound detected no heartbeat, in fact. The technician told your mom, "We're sorry, there's no heartbeat. You can have a D&C or let the miscarriage happen naturally."

Your mom decided to forgo a D&C. Your parents spent a couple of weeks grieving the pregnancy, but your mom, while she continued to have light bleeding, also continued to have pregnancy symptoms. A follow-up ultrasound showed your little heartbeat thumping on the screen, hard and fast. Your mom cried and your dad announced, "There's our little Pea."

Stubborn and strong, then and now.

Every time he calls you Pea, you imagine rolling a tiny hard pit with your tongue and you choke at the thought. It's come to that. Imagining that small piece of vegetable caught in your throat, this name he calls you, you choke it down, feed it to the monster. You cringe.

"Hi Dad."

Your dad is Vice President of Athletics at a local university, and when he's not focused on sports at work, he's focused on them at home.

And right now he's where he always sits. In the family room, the TV set to ESPN, watching a game. It's not important what kind of game, just that it's a sport.

You used to think your dad was the most handsome man in the world, a prince. He was so big and strong and you thought he could save you from anything.

He tilts his head in your direction.

"How's that new friend of yours?"

"Ben?"

"The track star," he says.

It's the only way he's going to remember him.

"He's fine," is all you offer.

"He didn't try anything funny the other night, did he?"

"Don't worry. He didn't even kiss me." You've given your dad the answer he needed to hear, the truth.

Ben hadn't tried to kiss you after the movie. He asked if you were hungry. You weren't, but you shrugged and said, "Whatever you're up for."

You went to Jimmy John's and he asked if you wanted

anything, and while you were scared to be in an eating environment with Ben, you said maybe you'd have some of the chips that he got with his sandwich. You felt like you could eat chips. You talked about the movie and you fed the monster some of Ben's salty chips. Because no matter how much you hate the monster, he's important. You take care of him because he tells you to. It's that simple.

The two of you ate, and you talked, and you looked into each other's eyes. When your hair got stuck on your lips, Ben moved his fingers slowly across your cheek, touching your face.

"Your hair," he said. "It's . . ." Then you shook your head to move your hair away and laughed.

"I like it when you laugh," he said.

So you laughed again.

You laughed all night. Somehow you made him laugh all night too.

When he dropped you off, he rushed out of the car before you could get out and went to your side to open the door for you.

"Wow," you said.

"What?" he said.

"I'm just not used to being treated this way."

"What way?" he asked.

"Like I'm special."

"Get used to it, because you are."

Your knees got a little wobbly. He took your hand, squeezed

it, then rubbed your palm gently, as if you already had a secret hand-holding ritual. It was no less spectacular each time. In fact, it started feeling more spectacular the more he held it. Every time he touched you, you felt like you were spectacular.

At the door, he took both of your hands into his and put his forehead to yours.

"Hey," he said.

"Hey back."

"This was a great date," he said.

"Yeah." It came out sort of like a whisper from a dream that you didn't want to wake from.

"But you know what?"

"What?" you asked.

"The next one is going to be way better."

He squeezed your hands in an urgent kind of way like he wanted to not leave, like he wanted to do what you were dying for him to do—lean in, tilt his head, and put his lips on yours. You wanted to smell him that close, to breathe him in, to know what it would feel like to kiss him for the first time.

But you knew it wasn't going to happen, and that was okay. Because you'd never get that first kiss back, and you knew it would be one of those first kisses that you were going to want to put into a box and take out every day of your entire life to relive over and over again.

Your foreheads were still touching and you stood like that for what seemed like forever. You didn't want to move. There were outside night noises: crickets chirping, a sprinkler going off, and the neighbor's dog barking. You thought you heard Ben's heartbeat, but then you realized it was your own heart beating out of your chest.

He put his warm lips to your forehead and you felt the sensation course through your body like an electric wave.

Just as quickly as it happened, he moved his lips away. You looked up at him, and you must have seemed desperate. You didn't want to be desperate.

"I'm going to text you as soon as I get home, okay?" he said.

"Yeah."

10

It's late Monday afternoon and you and your mom meet with Shayna for your first one-on-one therapy session. Normally, your mom won't be here, but for this first meeting, Shayna suggested she be present. The plan is that every Monday, you'll have your one-on-one with Shayna, then you'll have a fifteen-minute break, and then, down the hall, you'll attend group therapy for girls with eating disorders. That's the part that has you nervous, but you have to commit to this. Mondays are going to suck.

On Thursday when you and your mom met with Shayna for the first time, she did a series of tests. She now explains to you both that you were born with very few taste buds, where a normal person has hundreds.

"Also," Shayna says, "I could tell that the insides of your cheeks are very sensitive, which must make chewing, tasting, and swallowing extremely unpleasurable to you?"

"Yes, it really is," you say.

"Well, what you have is ARFID." Shayna presents this diagnosis to you and your mom like she's offering you a gift, like this is an amazing announcement.

You shake your head in confusion, and your mom asks, "What's ARFID?"

"ARFID stands for Avoidant/Restrictive Food Intake Disorder and it means there's a feeding or eating disturbance *not* due to anorexia or bulimia, and *not* caused by self-esteem issues. It means you cannot tolerate many foods and may gag when presented with new foods. You have a small bank of 'safe' foods you are comfortable eating. And we know there is probably some psychosocial interference involved. My guess is that you don't do well in social situations where food is at the center of the event?"

You want to cry in relief that she has discovered your problem. This feels like a big win. It still doesn't make you want to try to eat new things, but at least it's an explanation of why you're the way you are.

Your mom asks a bunch of questions about treatment and Shayna tells her that she's helped others with ARFID, and that she feels confident she can help you too.

"I can't believe we finally have a diagnosis," your mom says. "For so long, we've been going to nutritionists and different doctors, trying to find out what was wrong. When they look at her they think she's fine."

"That's the thing about ARFID," Shayna says. "Most people

with ARFID look perfectly okay, and since it's a newly named disorder, not many professionals are familiar with it, or even know the best way to treat patients."

When your hour with Shayna is up, your mom hugs you and thanks Shayna. To you, she says, "I'll come back to get you. Good luck with your next session."

You felt that your session with Shayna went well but when you walk into group therapy, your heart starts racing because the room is filled with a bunch of girls and they're all staring at you, the new kid. You feel completely out of place as you take a seat on one of the couches.

Immediately you think you don't belong here with the anorexics and bulimics. Shayna said your disorder isn't like theirs—and you want nothing to do with these girls.

Suddenly, you're mad at your parents for sending you here. You're mad at Shayna, who said she was going to help you. You feel as if she's got it all wrong now. You know these girls are looking at you and coming to their own conclusions about you. It feels like a clusterfuck.

And then, just when you thought it couldn't get any worse, it does.

Shayna introduces you to the group and tells them you are there not for anorexia or bulimia, like the rest of them, but for this newly named eating disorder called ARFID.

"Basically, it means she only eats a few foods," Shayna explains.

"So she's just like a *picky eater*?" a very thin girl says.

You knew it. It's that picky-eater thing you've heard a hundred times before, and so you stare down the girl. You fucking hate it in that room. You are not going to speak during the whole freaking time you're here.

You hate the whole fucking world at that moment.

But then Shayna sticks up for you.

"No, it's more than that. ARFID is extremely serious. It can evolve into purging and bingeing and even become a serious medical problem. Many ARFID patients can become anorexic or bulimic. Psychologically, it can cause extreme anxiety and depression and other social or mental disorders as well. It's lucky that she got here when she did."

"How come no one's ever heard of it before?" someone else asks. You're not looking at anyone because you're so over it.

"Well, the disorder has been around forever. But it's just been named, so in that way it's fairly new. It's a disorder that's affected by trauma, like with you all, and ARFID can be triggered at very young ages. So, as always, with new members, I want to remind you that this is a judgment-free zone and I ask you to be kind."

This is when you look up and see eight sets of eyes on you. Some of the girls smile lightly, some look beaten down, some look exhausted—they look like how you feel. You wonder if they have monsters, and how bad their monsters have been to them. You wonder if they hate eating. You wonder if they feel happiness, or sadness, or pain and anger. You wonder if they like how food tastes, or if they have cravings, or if they feel hunger. You're sure they feel some of these things. You wonder what they're like, if they sit in their rooms listening to sad music in the afternoons, trying to figure out what went wrong. You wonder if they wonder, like you do, what they did to deserve this life. You wonder if they cry at night when the lights go out because that's the only way to quiet the monster inside them.

You pull your stare back down to your lap, quieting the wonder in your body, quieting the questions in your mind. You guess you'll have to wonder some more, at least until they figure out how to help you kill this monster.

11

Ben asked you what you wanted to do, and you really didn't care, as long as you got to be with him, but you didn't want to say you didn't care because that would make you sound boring and that had been one of the problems with Alex, so you suggest putt-putt golf. He comes to get you and he opens the car door for you again, and you're hit with Abercrombie & Fitch and clean soap all over again.

You breathe.

You can't believe this perfect boy likes you.

The two of you have texted every night, you've been on Face-Time, and Ben's been over to your house too, but this is your official second date. One night he came over and you ended up watching one of the *Scream* movies on Netflix. You held hands, but nothing more than that happened. You were nervous most of the night, partly because you were jumpy from the movie and partly because you were afraid he might kiss you. Of course, you want him to kiss you, but your parents were home and that wouldn't have been cool–to have your mom or dad walk in on a make-out session.

Another time, Ben "stopped by" because he was in the neighborhood. Surprisingly, you didn't freak out when you answered your door in Victoria's Secret PINK sweats and no makeup. You figured you met on a day when you had no makeup on, and your hair was as raggedy as it would ever be–you had river-rat hair that day–so if he likes you after seeing you like that, then he really must like you for you. Which gives you a boost of confidence and you want to make sure to hold on to that. Because you think that for once someone, this someone, Ben, likes you for who you are. Even though you've got the monster inside you.

You're going to tell Ben about the monster tonight. You're scared he might not like you after you tell him there's something wrong with you. And that things might turn out like they did with Alex, not that you ever told Alex–things just got out of control with him. But now you're trying to get help, your parents are getting you help, and Shayna is trying to help you too. You need to tell Ben something, and soon, if you're going to be together. You're just not sure what to say: *So I have this monster?* or, *I don't eat much?* Either way, sharing this big part of yourself with him is a scary idea.

At Majestic Mini-Golf, Ben pays for the eighteen-hole course, then grabs two putters. He chooses an orange ball and you choose a green one.

"I thought you would have picked a pink or yellow ball," he says.

"Why?" you ask.

"I don't know. Maybe that's what I expect girls to do, pick girlie colors, but you're different. I should have known better. That you'd pick the unexpected color."

"Well, green is my favorite color, so I wanted the green one," you say.

"Aren't you feisty tonight," Ben says, laughing.

You feel good around him. Ben makes you want to be yourself.

On the eleventh hole he wraps his arms around your waist, pulls you close to him, so close you can smell the gum on his breath, and whispers in your ear, "I would love to kiss you."

There is a family waiting impatiently behind you for their turn. Neither of you wants your first kiss to be on the eleventh hole while an annoying family waits their turn for putt-putt. The moment is lost, and you move on to the twelfth hole. But something's changed. He looks at you more intently and touches you carefully as you maneuver through the maze of windmills and castles to finish the course. You wonder what's next.

You can't wait for what's next.

Your whole body buzzes.

You shove the monster far down. You're not telling Ben about him tonight.

You can't.

12

Ben buys milk shakes for the both of you, and then he drives down the highway.

The milk shake is vanilla. It's safe. You like chocolate too, but vanilla is good. You didn't realize how hungry you were, and when the cold, creamy froth makes its way down into your stomach, the monster growls his approval. Usually you don't think about the last thing you ate, and now you remember it was breakfast; you had half a chocolate-chip muffin and a glass of Carnation Instant milk. This milk shake is heaven. Being with Ben is heaven.

You slurp through the straw and ask, "Where are we going?" You really don't care, because you're in the car with Ben, and you're drinking a milk shake, and the monster is satiated. Really, there's nothing to worry about. Things at the moment are pretty perfect.

"You'll see," he says.

And because it's Ben, and you already trust him, you trust him.

Ben pulls off the highway onto a gravelly semi-road and you tell yourself to still trust him. There are cacti everywhere, which isn't unusual, but you're really in the desert and you know if you get too far out, there are some serious wild animals. Where you live, the wildest animals you encounter are Todd and his dick friends.

"What if there are like javelinas or coyotes or bobcats out here? What about rattlesnakes?" you ask.

"Don't worry," he says, and laughs.

Then you think that you haven't known Ben that long, and even if he is hot and looks and smells like an Abercrombie model, should you really be okay with this? Your heart starts thumping at a faster pace.

"Why are we driving this far into the desert?"

"It's okay. We're going to go watch shooting stars," he says. Then he tilts his head toward you. "Did you think . . . ?"

"Well. What was I supposed to think?"

The road is bumpy and Ben has stopped the car. He turns toward you and grabs your hand. "I'm sorry. I didn't mean to make you nervous. You okay? I thought this would be nice, you know, kind of romantic."

You laugh quietly, a bit embarrassed, and say, "Okay." You can't believe he's planned a romantic date.

You see a sign for the trailhead of Lone Dog Mountain, a trail you and your family used to hike when you were little, when you didn't mind hiking. Now that you know where you are, you feel more relaxed.

"Oh, we're at Lone Dog?" you ask.

"Yep. Come on," he says. He grabs a blanket from the backseat and you both get out of the car. Ben pulls you toward him and puts his arm around you.

The night is pitch-black but the sky is bursting with stars. Ben suggests sitting on some rocks at the trailhead but you say no because you're sure there are rattlesnakes and scorpions. But there is a visitors' center so you point and say, "Let's sit there."

Since the trail closes at sunset, the night is still and quiet, except for the sound of water trickling from somewhere. Ben uses the light from his phone to guide you to an open area where a water feature sits beyond the visitors' center. Surrounding the fountain are six large concrete benches in a hexagon shape that are almost too big to even call benches. You imagine dozens of children scrambling upon them during the day while tired parents rest after long hikes.

You and Ben sit side by side on one of the concrete benches, facing the fountain, and at first it's a bit awkward and uncomfortable because you're straining your necks upward to the sky, waiting for stars to fall. Then Ben says, "Here, let's try this," and he pulls you up.

He spreads the blanket out on the concrete bench and tells you to lie down on your back. Your heart is racing like crazy but you do this. Then he lies down, not next to you, although there is plenty of space for him to do that. Instead, he lies so the top of his head is touching the top of yours and his body is sprawled in the opposite direction of yours. He says, "Now, give me your hands." You reach your hands over your head and he reaches to touch your hands and you connect that way. You're both lying there, looking up at the sky.

"There," he says.

"There," you say.

"So," he says.

"So." You giggle.

"Are you copying me?" he says.

"Are *you* copying *me?*" you ask.

"Do you want to play a game?" he asks, moving his fingers along the length of your fingertips. He's doing this with both of his hands, to each of your fingers. It, of course, feels freaking amazing.

"What do you want to play?" you ask.

"Twenty questions, I go first," he says.

"Okay," you say.

"Um, favorite band?" he asks.

"Oh God, I don't know, like forever, or of the moment?" you ask.

"Ever."

"U2."

"Bonus points, right there," he says. "Favorite movie?"

"*Perks of Being a Wallflower*, also favorite book."

"Favorite flower?"

"Definitely white carnations."

"Not red roses?"

"So cliché."

"I knew I liked you. Okay, next question, best day of the week?"

"What's today?"

"Tuesday."

"Then Tuesday is the best day of the week."

"You are winning all sorts of points in this game," he says.

You pull your hands away from him and flip over so you're lying on your stomach. You settle onto your elbows because you're tired of looking up at the sky. You want to look at him.

He flips over too so you're face-to-face. He's got his elbows on the concrete, his chin in his hands, and he's staring at you.

"You cold?" he asks, and places his finger gently on your forearm.

"Is that one of your twenty questions?"

"Nah, just want to know."

You feel cozy and not one bit cold even though the temperature has dropped. "I'm okay," you whisper.

"I have another question I just thought of," he says.

"Yeah?"

"Can I kiss you now?"

You swallow hard and close your eyes, and when you do, images of the stars from the sky flash before you, all purplish, black, and silvery white. You feel movement and you open your eyes. Ben is inching forward on his stomach, and then his hand goes to your shoulder and his lips touch yours, and he's kissing you softly and you're kissing him back. It's perfect and it tastes like you thought it would—like peppermint from his gum and chocolate from his milk shake and a little bit salty sweet. It's cool, not hot, and he doesn't shove his tongue into your mouth the way Alex did. He just glides it across the inside of your mouth gently, exploring you a bit. He knows how to kiss, and it's slow and fabulous and you make a noise that sounds like a soft, happy cry.

After a few moments he pulls away but he's still holding on to your shoulder. You want to tell him not to stop, because you've never felt like this. You've never had this feeling in your life, and you feel like you could burst. You never want to leave this boy ever. You don't know how you're going to say good night to him when the date is over. You don't know if you're going to be able to do it.

You catch your breath. You're smiling at him. He's doing the same, smiling at you.

"It's my turn to ask you a question," you say finally. Your heart is racing from his kiss.

"You want to play the game *now*?" he asks.

"Yes."

"Really?"

You nod.

"Okay." He sighs. You can only imagine what he's thinking.

"Okay, here's *my* question . . ." You pause, and then: "Will you kiss me again?"

13

You're at the dinner table. You and your monster. You are trying.

You're rarely at the dinner table. You make up excuses, telling your mom you have a stomachache or that you ate already, or that you're just not hungry. Or sometimes you sit at the kitchen counter while your family eats and you pretend to eat, or you watch them eat, not even pretending to eat.

But tonight you're sitting with everyone: Your mom. Your dad. And your brother. He's not wearing his earbuds.

There are steaming bowls of food on the table. Corn. And some mashed potatoes speckled with pepper, and a big splat of butter melting in the center. There are rolls, and you know those are good. You will eat those.

There's also a plate of grilled chicken. And some fruit. A mixture of slimy fruit. The colors are pretty–pastel and . . . well, fruity looking. You bet they might smell like they taste good, but you never get close enough to know for sure. Apples are the only fruit you actually like. But your mom didn't even think to put apples on the freaking table—the one fruit you would actually eat.

You have a drink. Water. Shayna says you need to drink more water. That you're going through most days dehydrated. You told her you drink water. That you drink like three glasses a day, and you drink milk. And soda.

"Soda doesn't count as your water intake," she told you at therapy.

Still. It's liquid. In your mind, that counts.

Shayna told you she was "in recovery" too. Like for the past fifteen years. What the hell does *that even mean*? You don't want to be in recovery for the rest of your life. You want someone to kill the monster, slice his head off quick and easy, with a machete or in a big ceremony in the center of town, complete with a guillotine, and get rid of the bastard once and for all.

"Can I get an apple?" you ask.

Your mom smiles at you. Hell, she's *beaming*. You would have thought you'd asked for a steak.

You get up and grab an apple, the peeler, and a knife. You won't eat the apple skin. Because that's like people skin. You can't do it.

You come back to the table and your dad and Todd are already digging in.

"How are your seven a.m. practices going?" your dad asks

Todd. He's on the varsity football team and practice has started even though school doesn't begin for two more weeks. It's all they ever talk about. Sports. Football. Sports. It's annoying as freaking freak.

"Mmm," Todd replies, his mouth full of dead chicken. The thought that the stuff in your brother's mouth used to have a beak and feathers and flapped its wings and probably laid eggs makes your stomach churn. The thought that it used to cluck on a farm and that children's nursery rhymes are written about the very thing your brother is chewing makes you want to run to your room and scream for hours.

"Gross," you say. "Don't talk with your mouth full."

"You should try it sometime," Todd says back to you. "This food-in-your-mouth thing. It's pretty good."

"Kids, please. Stop," your mom says. "I would just like to try and have a nice family meal for once. Please."

She's tensing up already, you can tell. She reaches for her wine and takes not really a sip, not quite a chug, more like a big swallow.

You grab a roll, put it on your plate, and start to peel your apple. Slowly. Everyone knows you're stalling. You know you're stalling. Your dad and Todd look your way and your brother rolls his eyes. You do your best to ignore him. You're waiting. Just waiting. You take a sip of your water. Your mom cuts her chicken and takes a bite.

There are brown spots on your apple.

"Can I get a different apple?" you ask your mom.

"If you eat some chicken," Todd says, laughing in your direction.

"Shut up," you say to him.

"Stop," your mother says. Your dad keeps eating.

No one has answered you yet. You ask again, "Can I?"

"Yes," your mom says.

You go to the fridge and choose a better apple, then come back to the table.

"How's that Ben kid?" your dad asks.

"He's good," you offer, and start the slow process of peeling your new apple.

"I don't like him," Todd says.

"You didn't even meet him," you say. "What do you care anyway? You don't even like *me*," you accuse.

"True," he says.

Your mom picks up her plate and wineglass and takes them to the sink.

"What, Mom?" Todd asks.

"I'm not going to sit here and listen to my children talk to each other like this. I try. I try so goddamn hard, and this is what I get." She is near tears, and you feel bad. You look down at your plate. You pick at your roll, place a piece of the bread on your tongue, like it's communion.

Your mom looks from you to Todd and back at you. Then she looks at your dad.

"Well? Are you going to do anything about these children?" she asks him as if he has an answer.

Your dad shrugs, shoves a forkful of potatoes into his mouth. Your mom lifts her wineglass, looks at the three of you, finishes the wine, and walks out of the room.

The monster has won again.

14

Can I see you tonight?

You're surprised when you get the text from Ben because it's Saturday night and he left last night to go camping with his family for the weekend.

You're home?

Yep, bad weather up north.

Would love to see you.

Can I come by in 15?

Sure!

You were supposed to see a movie with Jae but she bailed on you at the last minute so you had been in your room watching YouTube videos and sketching a bit with your drawing pencils. You change out of your sweats and pull on jeans and a cute T-shirt, one that's not been on your floor for weeks. You swipe on some mascara and paint your lips a glossy rose-petal pink. You sniff your armpits and spritz on some body spray for an added touch. You don't want to look like you're trying too hard, but you want to look like you care. There's a delicate balance.

You find a pair of socks on the floor, smell them, and decide they'll make the cut, but barely. Then you pull on your hot-pink Chucks and head downstairs.

"I'm going out with Ben for a little while," you announce to your parents, who are watching TV in the family room.

"Oh, are you?" your mother asks, and you know what she means.

"May I go out for a little while?" you ask, rolling your eyes.

"Where are you going?" your dad wants to know.

"I don't know," you say. "He just texted to see if I could go out. It's not a major deal." You're giving him all sorts of attitude. "How come Todd never gets the third degree when he goes out?"

Your dad sighs. "Be safe. And be home by eleven."

"Eleven! It's already nine-forty-five!"

"Your attitude, missy," your mom reprimands.

"Good God," you mutter under your breath. Then louder you say, "May I please have a little later?"

"Eleven-thirty."

The doorbell rings.

"He's here!" You turn to go.

"Eleven-thirty!" your dad reminds you.

"Bye!"

* * *

Ben's waiting for you on the front step and he gives you a huge hug.

"I'm so glad our trip got cut short," he says.

"Me too."

You haven't seen him since your date on Tuesday, the first time you kissed, and it's all you've been thinking about–kissing him again.

You get into the car and he doesn't ask where you want to go. You think you know what you both want to do so it's no surprise that you end up at the playground down the street from your house. He parks the car and turns off the engine and the lights.

"Hi there," he says, and moves closer to you.

"Hi."

"Thanks for coming out tonight."

"I totally wanted to see you."

"Same."

And then he is kissing you, and he pulls his fingers through your hair and his lips move across yours slowly, yet with purpose, and he's whispering your name.

"What?" you ask.

"I like you," he says so softly you can barely hear him. Then he says it again, a bit louder this time. "I really, really like you."

You can't hold back the smile you feel spreading across your face. "I really like you too."

You kiss some more and then you pull away from each other to take a breath, and you both laugh.

"So how was camping?" you ask.

"It was okay. I'm glad it ended up being only one night though. My dad loves it so we go a couple times during the summer to make him happy."

"I would hate camping," you say. "I've never been."

"You might not hate camping if you went with me." He lifts his eyebrows.

"Why's that?"

"Because we'd make it fun."

"I don't know. The thought of bears and snakes, and all that dirt. Sleeping on the ground. Not my thing."

"Are you a princessy girl?"

"No way! Come on! You know I'm not. But just, ugh. Too much nature and outdoors with camping."

"What about lakes?"

"Well, I happen to have met a great guy on a river once."

"Oh really? What about that?"

"Just some guy. So maybe I'm partial to rivers," you say.

"What if that great guy took you to a lake someday?"

"I'd consider it. As long as he cleared out all the snakes first."

Ben intertwines his fingers through yours and laughs. "I'll see what I can do about the lake snakes." He traces paths along your palm with his fingers and it brings goose bumps to your skin. You want to kiss him some more.

"What were you doing tonight anyway?" he asks. "I didn't take you away from anything important, did I?"

"Nope. Jae blew me off–we were going to go to the movies. I was sketching some stuff, not doing much of anything."

"You're really good at drawing, huh?"

"I pretty much love it. I wish I had more time for it."

"You'll show me your stuff sometime?"

"Of course," you say.

"Cool. Maybe I'll let you sketch me," Ben says, and turns his lips up into a grin.

"You mean, maybe I'll let you sit for a portrait sketch, because that's how it works." You laugh and kiss his nose playfully.

It's a great night after all, and just a short while ago you had been in your room watching YouTube and drawing, but now you're here, in Ben's car, kissing and talking and laughing, and there's nowhere else you'd rather be. He makes you happy. You think he brings out the best parts of you. You think you want this boy to stick around.

You hope he'll stick around. You hope the monster won't get in the way.

15

It's Monday and you and Shayna have finished your one-on-one session and it's time for group. There's a spot open on the couch near a girl whom you met briefly last week but you don't know if she's nice or not, because you didn't get a chance to know anyone. You still don't want to be here. Well, it's not like you don't want to be here; you know you have to do something to figure out how to get rid of the monster and nothing has ever worked before, and you think this might be the only way to get him to leave.

But it's stupid really, being here with these girls. Because you're sure none of them can relate to you or what you've been through or this eating thing you have, this ARFID. You didn't say anything at the first session, you just listened to them talk about their "relationships" with food. How much they love food, how they need food, how they are addicted to food. The bulimics anyway. Then there are the anorexics, who also love food but don't love what food does to their bodies, so they reject the food and choose to starve themselves in order to waste away to practically nothing.

You decide that to get this process started, you're going to have to share your feelings with them. Because isn't that what group therapy is all about? So when it's your turn to speak, you lift your head and clear your throat.

"I'm not like any of you," you start, and every single one of them shifts in her seat. Their body language moves to defensive positions. Hailey, the worst of the bulimics, the one who binges on Oreos and pancakes, who hides candy bars in her sock drawer, who purges everything she puts into her mouth, says, "That's bullshit. Your parents wouldn't have brought you here if you weren't *exactly* like us." She crosses her arms over her chest and nods to the other girls, waiting for them to say something, anything to agree with her.

Shayna says, "Hailey, judgment-free. That sounds like an assumption to me."

"I'm just stating the obvious," Hailey responds snidely to Shayna.

When no one backs Hailey up, you speak again.

"Well, I have never, *ever* in my entire life looked forward to eating food. I have never in my life thought, 'Oh, I cannot wait to have a piece of pizza or a burger,' or, 'I'm so excited to go out with friends for dinner.' Now, there are times when I'm hungry, of course—we all have to eat to survive—but unless it's one of my safe foods, I don't care about food." You search the eyes of every girl in the room. And you continue.

"And Shayna says that ARFID can stem from trauma in utero. My mom thought she miscarried me. That's the trauma that probably started my whole disorder, as science-fiction as it sounds. You guys, from what I heard last week, have had traumatic experiences at older ages, like divorce or abuse, or something bad happening later. And that's awful, and I'm so sorry that happened to you. But you used to be able to eat normally before you had your disorder. You used to sit down with your family and have a regular meal and talk about your day and be able to put stuff on your plate and chew and not think about what was in your mouth. But I *never ate normally*. I don't know what it's like to want to eat normally. I don't know what it's like to desire food. You guys, at one point, have desired food. Maybe you still do? I don't."

You're mad and frustrated and also emotionally drained from admitting all of this and then one of the girls nods in agreement, and another girl gives you a thumbs-up. Shayna smiles big and bright and you look around the room, stunned. You totally called them out, and were not so nice about it, telling the girls that your stuff was more serious than their own problems, and that they didn't understand what you were going through.

"Very, very good," Shayna says. "Thank you for processing your feelings with us today. I know that was hard for you."

You can't believe these girls aren't pissed at you. They're actually okay with what you said? This is what group therapy is all about?

What the hell is going on here?

16

Jae's sitting on your bed next to you and the two of you are watching YouTube on your Mac. You've been hanging out for hours, streaming videos on makeup, hairstyles, and how to do your nails. You've also watched a couple of those stupid You-Tube challenges, like how many food items you can put in a blender and drink without puking.

You hit Mute on the blender food challenge when the girls in the video start gagging while drinking a mixture of oysters, avocado, chicken wings, ketchup, soy sauce, milk, and Hershey's syrup.

"How can you watch this video when you can't even eat?" Jae asks.

If you think about it, even a blender challenge with milk and strawberries would put you into cardiac arrest. Those little seeds in the strawberries–you cannot even fathom. The monster won't let you.

"No idea." You close your Mac.

"Does Ben know yet?" she asks.

You know what Jae means and she's trying to be helpful; she's not interfering at all. So you tell her how you wanted to tell Ben about your food problems at putt-putt golf, but that it didn't happen. "It wasn't the right time," you say.

"You should tell him," Jae offers kindly. "You don't want another Alex situation on your hands."

"I know." And while you appreciate the fact that Jae cares about you, you also want to change the subject. "Oh! Get this! Ben said he'll watch *The Fault in Our Stars* with me sometime."

"*The Fault in Our Stars*, really?" Jae asks.

"He says he wants to see it."

"What guy wants to watch *Fault in Our Stars*?" Jae says.

"I know," you say.

"Wow."

You fall back onto your pillow. "Yeah, wow. Oh my God, kill me. I sound *so* basic," you say.

"But seriously, is he just like, everything?" Jae asks.

"Pretty much," you say.

Jae has never had a boyfriend, nothing serious, and you're pretty sure it's getting serious with you and Ben. You're pretty sure you want it to be serious.

It's just that Ben seems to get you, at least what you've shared of yourself. The times you've spent together, you've laughed and joked, and he understands your sense of humor and there's never a lack of words–you pull from each other, like magnets, and there's always something inside his head that you want to learn about, that he wants to share, that you want to know from him.

And the kissing, the kissing has just been . . . You can't stop thinking about the kissing. It stops the frenzy you feel about life, but it also brings up a storm of, you don't know what. It's like a nice, beautiful storm. A storm where you want to sit outside and watch the clouds roll over the sky. The kind that you know will roll in and not cause any damage, just a pitter-pattering of rain to clean away the dirt, refresh everything, and then the skies will shine bright again. Kissing Ben is that kind of storm.

You're both quiet for a while, then you open your Mac to turn on some music and Jae asks, "Do you think you'll do it with him?"

"Oh my God! I don't know."

Because you don't. You haven't thought of that. Not yet. You're only sixteen but Ben's almost seventeen, and you know practically everyone does it by the time they're your age. Sure, you've thought about sex, but you haven't thought about actually doing *that* with Ben yet. You just know you want the first time to be with someone you love.

"I haven't been seeing him for that long," you say. "Do you think *he's* done it before?"

"How would I know?" she asks.

"I don't know. He's friends with your cousin. He would know. Aren't they like pretty good friends?"

"I guess."

"And you're really close to your cousin. You could text Braden and ask him."

So Jae texts Braden, and you watch as the words fill her iPhone:

> Hey cuz, is Ben a virgin?

You watch as the three little dots fill the space as Braden types his reply:

> Bro code. Tell his gf I say hey.

On the one hand you're bummed out because you didn't get the info you wanted, but then you squeal a little when you see he calls you Ben's girlfriend. This means Ben's been talking about you to his friends.

"Shit," Jae says.

"I know, right! I'm his girlfriend!"

The next night your parents plan to go out and Todd's heading to some football party. You ask if Ben can come over to watch *The Fault in Our Stars*.

"I don't like the idea of the two of you in the house alone," your dad says.

Shayna has started discussing interpersonal skills in your one-on-one therapy and how to ask for what you want, so you try this new skill out on your dad. "You could stay home too then?" you suggest.

This is a first and it takes him by surprise. He doesn't say anything right away and then you wonder if he'll change his plans and actually stay home with you and Ben. The idea of the three of you watching *The Fault in Our Stars* has you thinking insane thoughts. You would rather eat a full chicken dinner than have to sit there with Ben and your dad watching the movie.

Finally, your dad wavers. "No funny stuff, Pea."

Your mom comes out of her room wearing a nice dress and attaching a set of new dangling earrings to her ears. "What's going on?" she asks.

"Pea wants to have Ben over while we're out."

"You sure that's a good idea?" your mom asks.

You roll your eyes super-dramatically at your mom to convey your annoyance. But because you don't want to make your parents angry, you don't say what you really want to say to them, and instead, you simply say, "Seriously, we're *just* going to watch a movie." And then you tell your mom she looks nice. Because she does.

They leave and Ben comes over. Right away he kisses you. Your back is against the front door and he keeps kissing you, pressing his body against yours. Your mind is all over the place—the kissing is amazing and it's all you want to do with him the whole night. His hands are in your hair. You used to wear it up in a hair tie because it's so thick and unruly that it can be hard to manage, but since Ben, well, since Ben you've been wearing it down. Because there is nothing, nothing like having a boy, particularly a boy who looks and smells and kisses like Ben, take his hands and pull his fingers through your hair while he is kissing your lips. And there is nothing, and you mean nothing, like having a boy like Ben move his lips to your ear and kiss you right below the earlobe and then whisper to you, "Hey."

It's one word, and it really has no meaning, but it's everything.

It is everything.

When you're with Ben, everything is perfect.

You pull away and you are not quite nose to nose because he's so tall, but you look up at him and you whisper back, "Hey."

17

You've already seen *The Fault in Our Stars* and you've read the book twice. You saw the movie in the theater with Jae and you clung to each other and bawled your eyes out. Now though, you're curled up on the family room couch with Ben, and the end scene with Hazel Grace has just played.

It's the first time he's seen the movie.

"Well, that was a buzz kill," he says.

"What do you mean? Why?" you ask.

"Come on, her boyfriend died."

"Yeah, but it's the most beautiful movie ever," you say. "Don't you get it?"

"Not really."

You thought he would understand. Now you have to explain it to him.

"It's *perfect*. Don't you see? We already know from the beginning that Hazel Grace is going to die. And it's awesome that Augustus dies!"

"You're weird." He kisses your nose.

"But don't you *get it*?"

He shakes his head.

"She has terminal cancer. We *all* know it's going to happen. And then she meets Augustus, and she gets to experience love with him on earth, but he dies *before her*, so he's going to be there waiting for her when she dies. For all *we* know, Hazel Grace could die the next day!"

"Like I said," Ben says, "you're weird."

"Maybe you and I should go find John Green and ask him to tell us what actually happens to Hazel Grace? Even though *I* already know the answer."

"Do you have any ice cream?" Ben asks.

You click the TV off and uncurl your legs from underneath you. Ice cream sounds good. Ben follows you into the kitchen and you dig through the freezer and find your mom's stash of Ben & Jerry's.

"Do you want Cake Batter or Peanut Butter Fudge?"

"Peanut Butter Fudge," he says.

You pull both pints out and grab some spoons and hand him the peanut butter ice cream. When he opens it up he shows you its contents.

"Uh, what happened to the fudge core?" he asks. There is a hole dug right through to the bottom where the gooey middle is supposed to be.

"Guess my mom was having a bad day. It happens a lot."

You settle onto the kitchen counter and start eating the Cake Batter ice cream. He sits on the stool in front of you and digs into what's left of his pint like it's the best thing he's ever tasted. Then his gaze meets yours.

"Heard you and Jae texted Braden last night."

Your eyes go wide and you turn your head to avoid looking at him.

"What are you talking about?" you finally say, making eye contact.

"You know what I'm talking about." He takes another bite of the ice cream and twists the spoon in his mouth. You do know what he's getting at but all you can think of is how freaking sexy he looks while he eats ice cream.

"Well . . ." you say.

"Is there something you wanted to know about me?" He smirks.

"Jae brought it up," you admit.

"Jae brought what up?" You realize now he's teasing you and you relax. He puts the ice cream down and stands up from the stool. He places his hands on your knees. They're cold from when he held the ice cream but they feel nice.

You blurt it out: "Jae asked me if you've done it before and I told her I didn't know."

He kind of smiles sideways. It's really cute but you can't tell if it's an answer. You don't know if it means yes, he's a virgin, or no, he's not a virgin.

He takes the ice cream out of your hand and puts it on the counter next to you. He leans into you and starts kissing you. His lips are cold and he tastes like Reese's peanut butter cups. He puts his hand behind your neck and pulls you closer. You kiss for a while, and you get that feeling in your low abdomen where everything goes empty and swoops at the same time, that feeling like you need to be filled up. You don't know if you want to stop at just kissing.

After a while, he pulls away and looks into your eyes, his hand still on the back of your neck. You're glad you're not standing because your knees are weak.

"What were we talking about?" you finally say.

"If I've done it or not," he says.

"Yeah, that," you say.

"Here's the truth," he says.

"Okay?" You bite your lower lip, unsure of what you want the truth to be.

"I've had girlfriends, and I've done some stuff. But not that. There hasn't been anyone I've wanted to get close enough to. Yet."

He kisses you again, then picks up the ice cream and feeds you a bite of it. You don't feel the monster anywhere inside you.

Ben doesn't need to ask you the same question. Because you're sure he knows the answer.

18

The monster's been quiet, but he's there, lurking still. Lately though, he's been hiding in a dark corner, and you know it's because things have been pretty great with Ben. Actually if you were to describe what's happening with Ben, it would be way more than "pretty great." You've never felt this way about anyone.

Alex had been your first boyfriend, and now that you have Ben, you know that Alex meant nothing and only caused you pain. You don't want to give Alex the credit of calling him your first real boyfriend because with Ben you're discovering what a real boyfriend is. It's true, Alex was the first boy who paid attention to you, the first boy who wanted to kiss you, but he knew nothing about kissing. He was the first boy who held your hand in public, the first boy who declared your relationship a "relationship" back when Facebook was something. He was the first boy who met you at the movies, who kissed you in the back row in the theater, who made you think you had butterflies in your stomach.

Those weren't butterflies.

With Ben, you have butterflies. A flurry of them.

Now that you are experiencing what it's like to spend time with a boy who really gets you, who wants to be with you for you, you realize that Alex was nothing. And the difference between the way your mind and body worked then and now is worlds apart.

And the fact remains that Alex was also the boy who didn't understand that your mind worked differently when it came to eating, and thinking about food, and being around food. And while you can't completely fault him for that—because you weren't capable of explaining yourself or your problems to a fifteen-year-old boy—he made a pretty big mess of your life in the aftermath.

And while the monster's quiet now, you know he's there still, gnawing. Maybe he's sitting in the corner of your mind, rocking in a tiny chair, whittling away at you, like you're a piece of wood he's been carving at, trying to create something new, something that he wants to own. Yet somehow you're fighting it. Because if you're not fighting it, he would have won by now, right?

The gnawing: you try to ignore it. You're trying really hard. You're embracing what you're learning at Healthy Foundations. You're trying coping skills. Using them at home. With your parents, with Todd. Even though Todd treats you like you don't exist. You're hoping that one-on-one therapy with Shayna and group therapy will be the monster's demise.

You eat salad at another family dinner. Your mom glows and encourages you.

"Honey, that's wonderful. I'm so proud of you!" she says when you place a piece of lettuce in your mouth. You chew it and imagine you're chewing grass. Then you stab a crouton and eat that.

"Look, Mom," Todd says, "I took a bite of my lettuce too!"

You glare at him.

Your dad pierces his ham, rubs it into the potatoes, and shoves it into his mouth. Then he corrals some peas and wrangles those into his mouth too. You imagine all of that in his gut soon, churning away, mixing together, and the image is too much for you to take. Thinking about the colors and the textures of the food, and the smell of it all. But you push the gnawing monster back into the corner and you take a long sip of your ice water.

Cope.

Cope.

Cope.

Shayna is teaching you at therapy.

And even though you've only had group twice, you feel there was a crack in the surface with the girls last week, and they may be able to help you. Their eating disorders are different from yours, but the ways to cope are the same. They've all been in therapy longer than you have and you can learn from them if you give them a chance.

You smile at your mom. You really want to please her. She does mean the world to you. You know she's trying to help you.

Your dad finishes swallowing the chum in his mouth, and he speaks about something other than football for once.

"You kids ready for school to start?"

Not what you wanted him to talk about. But you guess it's a small attempt at something other than football.

"I can't believe I have a junior and a senior in high school." Your mom is too wistful.

Todd actually looks at you and rolls his eyes. You smile at him. It is a bonding moment the two of you haven't had in years. You are encouraged to take another bite of your salad. You chew. You stab a raw baby carrot and put that in your mouth. You've never been afraid of raw carrots. You're not sure why. Maybe it's the crunch they make when you put one between your teeth, or maybe it's the sweet tang of orange crisp you taste when you bite into one. But you've never feared carrots. Carrots are safe.

Your mom sips her wine. Your dad plows through some more ham chum. Todd starts talking about a hot chick he thinks he might want to "hook up" with this year.

"Todd!" your mother says, glaring at him. "Don't talk like that!"

Todd puts one earbud in his left ear, and you're pretty sure he's listening to some new rap artist. Your mom gets up and pours another glass of wine and your dad asks for more potatoes.

This is the most normal family dinner you've experienced in like forever, and you don't know what's happening here, but it's really weird.

You might kind of like it.

Is this what it's like to cope?

Is this how to kill the monster?

"Does anyone want to go get froyo after dinner?" your dad asks.

19

When Alex broke up with you, the monster made you stop eating. It was spring of sophomore year and you thought your world was over. Alex didn't understand how you couldn't eat in front of other people and you couldn't explain it to him. He wanted to go out with friends, you didn't want to be with other people. He got tired of you, of how you were. He didn't get it.

In the beginning with Alex, you thought everything was perfect. You held hands and kissed. You hung out at your locker. You texted all the time. You went to basketball games and movies–perfectly fine things to do that didn't involve unsafe foods. Normal stuff you're supposed to do when you get your first boyfriend.

Then the monster interrupted. He made you turn quiet. You couldn't explain to Alex why being at social events with food made you anxious. How you couldn't really eat much of anything, and how thinking about food made you sick sometimes, and how even, if you were in the wrong frame of mind, watching other people eat a hamburger could make your own stomach churn. Those kinds of things couldn't be explained, especially to a teenage boy whose second favorite thing to do was eat.

And so you started shutting down, shutting him out. You knew he liked you a lot. He really did. In the beginning, he liked everything about you. He told you that you were pretty. He told you that you were funny and nice. That he thought about you at night before he fell asleep. He told you so many great things. Things that a girl wanted to hear from a boy she really liked. You liked feeling important, and special, and like you meant something to somebody other than the monster.

Alex started to not understand. The way you were. Of course, you could go places with him. You could also manage to sometimes watch him eat a double cheeseburger with all that stuff on it—bacon and tomatoes and onions—and sometimes, if you could push the monster down far enough, you could stop your stomach from churning. And you could eat some French fries with him and pretend that everything was okay.

After a while, Alex felt like you weren't into him anymore. That's what he told you when he broke up with you—he felt like you weren't "into it, into him" any longer, which was the furthest thing from the truth. It wasn't that you weren't into him. That hadn't been it at all. It had been the monster the whole time, controlling everything you felt, and everything you did and wanted to do. It had been the monster that told you that you couldn't be normal around Alex, that you didn't know how to act normal, so it had only been a matter of time until he discovered this and got tired of you.

And, of course, as with anything in high school, everyone knew everyone's business, so everyone knew Alex dumped you. And although he broke up with you in the nicest possible way—and did it in person and not with a text—you still felt the hurt all the way through to your heart. Because after all, you thought you were in love with Alex.

And you stopped eating.

For five days.

On the fifth day, you fainted in Math class.

The rumors started.

This is what they said:

Alex broke up with her because she got pregnant.

She fainted and lost the baby.

She got an STD from someone so Alex broke up with her.

She's anorexic.

She cheated on him.

She's a lesbian.

They were all over the place, the things that were said about you.

Because not only did everyone see you faint in Math class, but everyone saw the ambulance that rushed you to the ER.

Your parents met the ambulance at the hospital.

The doctor put you in a room, gave you fluids through an IV, and you lay there, thinking if only you ate, things would be better. You would be better. You would have Alex back, you would have a life back.

You felt the monster cackling inside.

When the doctor came in and asked you what happened, you answered, "I don't know."

"You don't know?" he asked you.

"I fainted?" you said.

Your mom said, "I don't think she's been eating enough."

The doctor asked if you'd been eating, and you said, "My boyfriend just broke up with me so maybe I haven't been eating much."

He asked you a bunch of questions about your diet, and your mom answered them, saying that you drank milk and ate yogurt and you ate peanut butter but no meat. And that you also ate apples and carrots and sometimes salads. A nurse drew blood, and the doctor said you were a little low on potassium and iron, suggested you take a daily multivitamin, told your parents your body weight was perfect for your height and age.

Perfect.

There it was again. That word.

The monster inside laughed.

See, you're perfect.

Your parents sat with you while you were rehydrated and they pumped potassium through your veins. Your mom and dad thought you had fainted because you were depressed over the breakup. They had no idea you had not eaten for five days. In your mind, this was the monster punishing you, starving you, making you hurt. You deserved to feel the emotional and physical pain of your first real breakup.

You took the rest of the week off from school, but when you went back, the rumors were still swirling. People looked at you differently, whispered about you. Alex, who had said he wanted to "still be friends," avoided your glances. You felt alienated. Alone. Alone with the monster.

Jae stood up for you as best as she could, and by the end of the year there was a girl who actually did get pregnant, one of the girls with hundreds of thousands of followers on Instagram. The rumor was she got pregnant by someone she met online, so her news was bigger and more rumorworthy than what you had gone through, and kids stopped talking about you.

But while they stopped talking about you, it wasn't like they forgot about you, and you aren't exactly looking forward to school starting next week.

School with the monster.

20

You stop taking your little yellow pills. You decide you don't need them anymore because you're happy. You're finding ways to be happy and Ben is a part of this new feeling.

You started taking the pills after Alex. You were in a haze, going through the motions, barely doing what you could to get through the days to make it to the end of the school year, just to get to summer. If you could only get to summer. Make it to the last day of school.

Thank God for your mom then. She knew there was something more going on after Alex. While things were never right with the way you ate—there was always a push and pull with that—after you ended up in the hospital, your mom knew you weren't well and took you to your pediatrician.

"She's depressed. She's more than depressed. She's not functioning."

You sat on the white crinkly paper in your pediatrician's office, feeling like you were four years old, listening as your mother talked about you as if you weren't there. Your hair stringy and covering your face, because you didn't want to look at anyone, you didn't want to see anyone, you didn't want anyone to see you. You wanted to be invisible. The monster wanted you to be invisible. The monster wanted you dead.

Between your mother and your doctor, they decided you were severely depressed and that's when the little yellow pills became a part of your morning ritual. The pills got you out of bed. They got you into the shower in the morning. They made you wash your hair. They made you eat occasionally even if it was just half a piece of dry toast at your mother's insistence, or two pieces of apple at dinner.

The little yellow pills got you through the rumors at school. They got you through the stares from the girls in the halls who normally wouldn't look your way. They got you through Alex walking past your locker and avoiding your glance. They got you through final exams. They got you through the end of sophomore year.

And now, you have stopped taking the pills. You're trading Ben for the pills. At first, you simply forgot for a couple of days, then you realized you didn't feel much different, and that you felt good even though you hadn't taken your pills. So you skipped them. And you're still feeling moments of happiness more often than not. Despite the monster. You think the monster may be dying. You haven't heard much from him lately. Maybe you're learning how to quiet him. Maybe he'll go away.

Through therapy, although you know you haven't been in therapy all that long. But. You know you're trying.

Shayna is going to help you learn how to like food and you're starting to trust her and the process. One of the things she plans to do is reintroduce food to you through four of your five senses: through touch, sight, smell, and then, finally, taste. You'd be lying if you said you weren't scared about this part of therapy. It's food. And it's very unfamiliar to you.

But you want to be able to enjoy it someday. When you are older, you want to go to functions like weddings, parties, and business meetings and not feel socially awkward. You want to walk to the buffet table and thoughtfully consider the foods and select things that look delicious and pretty—foods that you know are healthy and that will taste good. You want your stomach to growl in anticipation of a good meal, and you want to feel that fullness that others describe after they've had Thanksgiving dinner, when they pop open their top button, thankful for a home-cooked meal.

You've never felt that way. You want to appreciate food. You do. You just don't know how. And you so badly want to learn.

21

It's Ben's birthday and he's decided he wants to spend the evening with you and that you're going to meet his family later in the weekend. This is a huge deal because although you knew it was his birthday you hadn't talked about doing anything together.

"We're going out tonight, you and me, okay?" he says when he calls you that morning.

"What about your family?"

"Sunday afternoon we'll go to my house and celebrate. You'll get to meet everyone, okay? I want to see you tonight," he says.

You get butterflies in your stomach when he tells you again that he only wants to spend his birthday with you. When you ask where he wants to go he says he'd like to go to a movie and dinner.

You and Jae had gone shopping earlier in the week to find a present for Ben and you finally decided on something simple: movie tickets, and a gift card to Nike. Then as a joke, at the bookstore you bought him a *Fault in Our Stars* key chain.

"He'll either love it or hate it," you told Jae.

"Well, then, you'll know how he feels about you when you see his reaction to the key chain," Jae said.

"That's true," you said, laughing.

But now you think that since he wants to spend his birthday with you, it's a pretty good sign that things are going very well.

When you tell your mom you're going out with Ben, she gives you a sideways glance and says, "You're seeing a lot of him."

"I guess so," you answer her.

"Don't you think you should be more focused on therapy and working through your other problems? And not spending so much time with him?"

"Mom, I'm totally doing therapy. And the only time I feel good is when I'm with Ben. He makes me happy. He makes me not think about the food crap, all the stuff that bothers me."

"I'm just thinking about what happened last time," your mother clucks. She actually *clucks* like a chicken when she says this.

"This is not like with Alex," you say. "Nothing like how it was with Alex."

"I just don't want you to get hurt again."

The two of you go to the movies and you beg Ben to let you pay since it's his birthday, but he refuses. "I asked you to come with me. I'm paying." He grabs you by the hand and kisses you full on the lips. You literally cannot believe how charming this boy is. You snuggle and kiss during the movie and only partially watch because there's nothing else you'd rather do (well, maybe, but you're in a movie theater). Near the end you whisper in Ben's ear, "Happy birthday."

He whispers back to you, "It's my happiest one yet." And he pulls you closer.

You feel so lucky to have met him.

When the movie is over Ben announces that he's starving and asks you what you feel like eating. The monster snickers.

"I don't care."

"You feel like pizza, Chinese, Mexican?" he asks.

You figure you can fake your way through pizza so you say pizza sounds good. You're starting to feel really anxious and try to remember some of the skills you've been learning in therapy but your mind goes blank. You feel a physical shift in your system when you walk into Angelino's Pizza and smell the strong odor of garlic. It doesn't seem to help that Ben is holding your hand when the hostess leads you to a cozy booth near the back.

Ben senses your mood has changed and asks if you're okay. You want to be okay. It's his birthday. You don't want to ruin this night for him, so you lie and say you just have a little stomachache.

"Do you want to leave?" he asks, but you can tell he is disappointed.

"No, I'll be fine," you say.

You want so badly to be fine. You want so badly to be good for Ben. You want so badly to be good for yourself. You need to do this. This is just another one of the steps you have to take. And it's only pizza. You can usually do pizza, minus the cheese.

The waitress comes over and you both ask for Sprite. She leaves to get your drinks and Ben asks if you know what you want to eat.

"I don't know."

"What kind of pizza do you like?"

"Usually just plain."

"What if we did half cheese and half sausage?"

"That's okay," you say.

When the waitress comes back, Ben orders the pizza.

"You okay?" he asks again.

"I'll be fine." Then you remember the gifts in your purse, so you tell him that you've got something for him and his eyes light up. You pull out the envelopes with the tickets and gift card and the small package that has the key chain in it. You also got him a card. He opens the movie tickets first.

"We could have used those tonight," you say.

"We can use them another time," he says, smiling widely at you. Next he opens the Nike gift card. You tell him it's not much but maybe he can buy a T-shirt or some new socks for when track starts.

"And this one"–you push the small package toward him–"is kind of a joke."

He opens the key chain and cracks up. It's got a goofy quote from the movie on it, one that you both had laughed at when you watched it together.

"I love it!" he says, and you believe him because he adds it to his keys right away and comes over to your side of the booth and gives you a kiss.

You kiss him back and it doesn't even feel weird to kiss him in public. You want to take a picture of the two of you because you don't have one of him yet so you pull out your phone and hand it to him.

"I want a picture," you say.

"Oh, you do, do you?" He's grinning like crazy.

"I do."

"I guess we could do that." He clicks on the camera on your phone, turns it in his direction, and starts clicking pictures of himself making silly faces. He takes a dozen or more pictures. You grab your phone from him.

"No! One of us!"

"Oh . . . you want a picture of the two of us? You should have specified. I need your phone back then."

You hand him your phone and he pulls you to him tightly, holding you low around your waist. "You smiling?" he asks.

"Duh," you say. "I'm with you, of course I'm smiling."

"Right answer."

Ben clicks the camera at your faces. He moves it in a bunch of different directions as he tells you what to do: "Silly face.

Dramatic. Sad. Now kiss me! Kiss me again! Pouty! Angry. Kiss me again!" He sets the phone down and puts both arms around you.

"Kiss me again! It's my birthday."

You push him away. "You're nuts!"

"Nuts about you," he says.

You scroll through the pictures together, choosing the best one to put on Instagram. "Hashtag it 'AwesomestCoupleEver,'" Ben says.

The drinks and the pizza come and the waitress sets everything down. Ben plants one more kiss on your lips before moving back to the other side of the booth. You're not sure how you're going to manage to eat a piece of cheese pizza without the cheese on it. But it turns out to be okay, because Ben talks about how sweet the gifts are and how much he appreciates you, and he says that you didn't have to get him anything, he's just happy that you're here. He eats three pieces of sausage pizza and you eat one piece of plain pizza but you scrape off the cheese and he either doesn't notice or is so kind he doesn't ask why you did that.

There's one more thing you have for him, and while it's not really a gift, this is the thing that, when you give it to him, you're baring your soul. You pull out an orange soda from your purse.

"For you," you say.

"You got me a Crush soda?" he asks.

"Yes."

"Why?"

"Isn't it obvious?"

He furrows his brow like he doesn't quite understand. Suddenly you're embarrassed: you thought this would be cute and funny, but now you actually have to spell it out for him when the writing is literally right on the can.

"Because, duh," you say, "I have a crush . . . on you."

"Ohhhh. I get it now."

"You do?"

"Yeah."

He smiles big at you and you grin back, feeling stupid and goofy and so very happy. Like you always feel when you're with Ben.

22

Ben picks you up on Sunday afternoon, the last Sunday of summer break. You're nervous about meeting his family, but also excited–he's mentioned his little sisters, nine-year-old twins–and he keeps saying how much they'll like you. You're also scared about the food part of the evening, and when you asked him about dinner, Ben said it would be casual, so you didn't say anything else. You can't believe you haven't told him yet. Jae was right. You should have talked to him about your problem by now. The monster chuckles quietly, deep within.

The first thing you notice is Ben's house is loud and full of activity. Music is blaring through speakers, and their puppy barks at you and nips at your ankles. You lean down and scratch the puppy's ears. Ben pushes the pup away from you, saying, "No, Earl," and you laugh. Because the puppy's cute and because Earl is a crazy name for a dog.

The atmosphere is different than at your house, than with your family. Your house is always full of quiet anticipation and stress. Just you, your mom (who's always filling up her wine-glass), your dad watching ESPN, Todd with his earbuds shoved into his ears, and then the monster. There's always the monster—whether he's quiet or not, you know he's still around.

Ben's mom greets you at the front door with a huge smile and gives you a hug, which surprises you. Your family doesn't hug. You stand with your arms at your sides as she pulls you close.

"Hello! Welcome!"

"Hi," you say shyly.

"We're so glad you could come over. Ben has been talking nonstop about you since you guys met."

"God, Mom. Embarrass me much," he says. Then he reaches for your wrist, lightly pulling you away from his mom and says, "Let's go meet my sisters."

His sisters and his dad are outside. The girls are in the pool, but when they see you and Ben, they scurry out and come over to you, each vying for your attention, and they get you a little wet.

"Hi!" one says.

"Hi!" says the other.

They are identical except they have different swimsuits on and while they both have long, sopping wet hair, one twin's hair is a little shorter.

"I'm Olivia!" says the one with longer hair.

"I'm Alana!" says the one with shorter hair.

"Tweedledee and Tweedledum," Ben says.

Alana sticks her tongue out at Ben.

"Are you Ben's *girlfriend*?" Olivia asks.

"Yeah, are you two boyfriend and girlfriend?" Alana asks.

You laugh it off and change the subject. "What grade are you guys in?"

"We're going into fourth grade!"

"That's awesome," you say.

"Are you eating dinner here?" Olivia asks.

"Yep, I am," you say.

"Will you sit by me?" Alana asks.

"No! I want her to sit by me!" Olivia shouts.

"Hey, she can sit by everyone," Ben says.

They both pull at your hands and look at your bracelets. "Can I try this on?" Olivia asks about the gold braided bracelet on your left wrist.

"Sure." You take it off but Ben grabs it before you can give it to his sister.

"Not now, you're soaking wet." He hands the bracelet back to you.

"You're mean!" Olivia shouts.

"Yeah, *Ben*," you say. "You're mean." And you laugh.

"Hey, can I braid your hair later when it dries?" you ask the girls.

"Yes!" they yell in unison.

"I can do awesome French braids, if you like."

"Yay!" they scream together, and jump up and down.

Ben rolls his eyes. "Come on, I know my dad wants to meet you."

The girls cannonball back into the deep end of the pool, screeching in delight.

"Okay, you totally won them over," Ben says.

"I think they're adorable," you say.

"I think you're adorable," Ben says, and he kisses you on the forehead.

One of the twins yells from the pool, "Ewww, Ben just kissed her!"

"K-I-S-S-I-N-G!" the other twin shouts.

Ben's dad turns his head from the grill as you both approach him.

"Welcome to the humble abode!" he says, smoke clouding his face. He waves it away with a hand towel.

"This is Dad," Ben says.

"Call me Dan. How do you like your burgers?" he asks you.

The monster growls inside and your body feels as if it might go numb right there on the pool deck.

But you've been feeling so good lately, you push him back down and try to remember some of the skills you've learned at therapy. You smile at Mr. Hansworth.

"I'm trying out a vegetarian diet these days," you say.

"Hey, no problem! I'm sure Kathy's got some veggies in there we can round up for you! Nothing to worry about. We're just happy you're here and you're keeping Ben out of trouble." He smiles kindly at you. "You kids run along and go do whatever it is teens do these days."

"Thanks Dad," Ben says.

"Nice to meet you, Mr. Hansworth."

"Dan," he says. "Please, call me Dan!"

Ben turns you toward the house and you start walking to the sliding glass door. "You didn't tell me you were a vegetarian," he says.

"Is that a deal breaker?" you joke.

He laughs. "No way. You should have told me when we got pizza the other night. I wouldn't have gotten sausage on it."

"Well, there's more I should probably tell you, and I probably should have told you sooner," you say. "Like. I don't eat much."

"What do you mean?"

You've made it inside the house and fortunately his mom is busy in the kitchen. You take a seat in the living room together.

"I'm in therapy for an eating disorder," you admit. It feels scary to tell Ben this, but it also feels important because he's someone special and you're going to need his support. You're mad at yourself for waiting until it's five minutes before you're supposed to sit down with his family for dinner for the first time.

"So can you eat? Do you like, throw up and stuff?" He doesn't ask to be unkind; you can tell he truly doesn't know what it means to have an eating disorder.

"No. It's not like bulimia. That's the throwing-up disorder. And I don't have anorexia, although you could consider me borderline, because I guess if I don't eat enough to keep healthy it could get bad. That's why I'm in therapy. I go every Monday—to one-on-one therapy and also group therapy. To try to change my eating habits and behavior."

"But . . . and don't take this the wrong way . . . you look great," he says.

God, you love this guy. You're so grateful for him. How can he be this amazing and wonderful and . . . and you just want to put your arms around him right this second and hug him because he's looking at you with such concern, like he really wants to understand what's going on. He's really listening to you.

"I have what's called ARFID. It's a disorder where I'm sensitive to foods, and avoid a lot of things and restrict foods that are not familiar to me. I'm really scared of trying anything new. Like I'll gag and practically vomit when I try a new food. So I'm in therapy to learn to like food."

"What can you eat? What *do* you eat?"

"I should have told you all this before you invited me to dinner. I'm so sorry."

"It's okay, I'll tell my mom. Come with me," he says. He pulls you up from the couch and takes you into his arms and holds you for a few seconds. "Don't worry. My mom will understand."

He grabs your hand and you follow him into the kitchen, where his mom is prepping a salad. "Mom, what's for dinner exactly?"

"Well, Dad's making burgers, and I'm making a salad. We're also having chips and some fruit. What's up? Do we have a food allergy?" She looks at you.

"Um, I . . ." You look to Ben for help.

He puts his arm around your waist. It feels very protective and loving. And it gives you the confidence you need: "I'm in therapy for an eating disorder and not too many people know. I just told Ben."

"Oh honey!" She reaches for you and gives you a hug and you burst into tears, right in their kitchen. They are tears of relief and sad tears too. It feels good to cry. Ben's mom rubs your back and tells you that it's okay to cry and you're very brave and you should be very proud of yourself for sharing that with her because she is sure it was a hard thing for you to do. You're sniffling on her shirt and then you laugh because now you feel silly about the whole thing so you pull away and wipe your eyes.

"I'm sorry," you say.

"It's okay, it's okay," Ben's mom says. "You're going to be fine."

"I'm so embarrassed."

"Don't be," she says. "But let's see, what can you have?"

You give her the quick definition of ARFID and between the three of you, you decide you can have a peanut butter sandwich, an apple, and some chips for dinner. All the tears are dried up when Dan, Alana, and Olivia come in.

You end up sitting in between the twins at dinner so you don't even get to sit by Ben, which is a bummer, but fortunately, Ben's mom got to Mr. Hansworth–Dan–before dinner was served so he is clued in to what's going on. But of course, once the girls see that you get to eat a peanut butter sandwich, they also want one. Mrs. Hansworth is so nice, she makes them sandwiches too. And Dan is so cool, he says, "Hey, this just means more burgers for Ben and me!"

After dinner, Mrs. Hansworth brings out a chocolate cream cake and lights the candles for Ben. "I can't believe my son is seventeen!"

"You're old!" Alana says.

"You should get married now, you're so old!" Olivia adds. "Hey, you two should get married!"

There is laughter and an off-key round of "Happy Birthday" and you all eat cake. Cake is never a problem with the monster.

Afterward, everyone sits in the family room and watches a Disney princess movie that you've never seen, but Ben has and he knows all the songs and actually sings them with his little sisters, which is the most precious thing you have ever witnessed. You are amazed at how incredible his family is. You thought you were falling in love with him, and then to meet his whole family and see how awesome they are, well, you are in it deep now.

You braid the girls' hair as you promised, and they take turns brushing your hair. Ben says he wants a turn so he sits on the couch and you sit on the floor between his knees and he runs the brush through your hair gently. Your back is against the couch, and you take your hands and put your fingers under the soles of his socked feet, which are toasty warm. He presses down on your fingertips lightly with his toes, and then he squeezes his thighs against your shoulders. He's still brushing your hair and it feels like something wonderful. The girls are snuggled up near you on the floor—Alana's head is in your lap and Olivia is curled up next to you on the other side with a pillow and a blanket. You let them play with your bracelets and you've never felt so comfortable and relaxed with a family, not even your own.

About halfway through a second movie, Ben's parents tell the girls it's time for bed so the twins hug you and ask if you'll come over again.

"Do you think Ben will invite me back?" you ask them.

Olivia says, "He better or we'll kill him!" and Alana says, "You're the best girl he's ever invited!"

You turn to grin at Ben and then hug the girls again.

His parents say good night too and take the girls upstairs to bed. Then you and Ben are alone. He moves your hair all to one side, leans down, and kisses your neck, right below your ear.

The goose bumps are explosive.

"You *are* the best girl I've ever invited over," he whispers.

When he takes you home, you kiss at the front door until you feel completely woozy and disoriented. Finally, he says he has to go or he doesn't know if he'll ever be able to leave. He pulls himself away from you, but he promises he'll talk to you later. When you get inside and lock the door, your phone buzzes. It's a text from Ben:

I miss you already

23

During your session on Monday with Shayna, you tell her that you've begun to open up to your boyfriend about your disorder. You feel proud of this accomplishment.

"I didn't try any new foods at his house last night," you tell Shayna, "but now he knows that I have ARFID and it didn't freak him out."

"That's great," Shayna says. "It's really important that those you care about and who care about you are in the know and support you during this journey. It's going to be tough."

Shayna asks you about the rest of your week and you share about your family dinner and how you ate some lettuce, which was not your favorite thing to do but you did it anyway. She asks about your anxiety levels during the week, and your mood and how things have been at home with your family. You're honest with her and it feels good to talk with her so openly. You also admit that you're not looking forward to school, and she says most of the girls in group feel the same way.

You're surprised when she looks at her watch and mentions that time is up.

"Take a little break and we'll meet up for group in fifteen," Shayna says.

You part ways, check your phone, and see that Ben texted you:

Just thinking about you. ☺

It brings a smile to your face. You text him a quick note letting him know you'll call him later and you head into group, feeling less nervous than the last couple of times you were there.

You take a seat on one of the couches and soon the girls are filing into the room. A couple of them nod at you, some say hi, and you say hi back. Shayna arrives and takes her seat on the main couch. When everyone has settled in and quieted down, Shayna clears her throat to begin group.

"Tonight, we'll be doing something a little different. We're going to talk about your fears. What scares you, what concerns you, things like that."

One of the bulimics, Hailey—yes, the one who tried to call you out during last week's session—says, "My biggest fear is a bag of Double Stuf Oreos."

You laugh because you think she's joking, and everyone else laughs too. Shayna says, "That might be funny to some of you, but maybe to Hailey that's a real fear. It's something for all of us to think about."

The room goes quiet and Shayna slowly looks around.

"I'll pass out some paper and pens, and what I'd like you to do is spend about fifteen minutes thinking–really consider this: What are your fears? Anything and everything. Afterward, if you'd like to, you can share."

The paper and pens are distributed and you stare at the blank sheet in front of you. You absolutely without a doubt know your number-one fear and that's the monster, so the first thing you write down is:

Monster.

You're slightly embarrassed to be sixteen years old and have your main fear be a monster, but that's what you've written. The next thing on your list:

Food.

You think some more. Everyone is scribbling away, lines and lines of fears. It's that easy for them? Why can't you think of more fears? But then, isn't it good that you're struggling with this task? *Think. Think. Think,* you think.

Meat.

School.

Not being liked at school/popular.

Rumors at school.

Alex.

Mom drinking.

Todd being a douche.

Dad not being enough of a dad.

(Wait, how is that a fear? Just write, don't think, this is your list.)

Ben not liking me anymore.

BEN NOT LIKING ME ANYMORE.

That is your biggest fear.

Forget the monster. You have a new biggest fear.

"Okay, I think that's enough time," Shayna says. "Who wants to share?"

You sink into the couch. You're not sharing this.

These are your fears, and yours alone.

24

You wake with the monster. It's the first day of school and he's nudging you, scratching at you like a dog that needs to be let out. You feel him there, in the back of your throat, whispering. You try to shove him down, but can't. You don't want to get up. You remember how school was last year. Ben won't be there with you. You don't have any classes with Jae, and you'll only see her at lunch. You don't know how you're going to get through the day.

You lie there for a while, listening to your alarm go off three more times. Once every five minutes you hear the annoying sound that you set—a tune called "Walk in the Forest." You wanted a melody that would lull you gently from sleep, but now, when you've listened to it four times in the last twenty minutes, it sounds like music straight out of a vampire movie. You imagine a thick forest and the vampire coming to get the stranded girl. You need to change the alarm. It's looming and desolate and you never want to wake up to it again. You feel like you never want to wake up again, ever.

Your mom comes into your room with that huge forced smile on her face.

"Honey? You getting up?" She's trying for you. If she smiles, she hopes it'll make you smile. It doesn't work but you say you're getting up, although you don't move.

"You'll be fine," she says. "You're doing great. Things will be great today."

You flip the covers off, make your way into the shower, and turn the water on as hot as you can stand it, wishing you could accidentally scald yourself. Third-degree burns from the shower and a trip to the ER sound better than school.

You dress in a T-shirt and shorts and a pair of sandals, and put on a quick swipe of mascara and some lip gloss, although that much makeup feels like a lot of effort. You pull your hair back into a hair tie. You don't really care how you look even though you and Jae discussed first-day-of-school outfits last week at length. You feel like the monster is trembling inside, surging, trying to get out, trying to do something big, yet you don't know what, you don't know how it's making you feel. Just that he's there, gliding along the surface, searching for a way out.

You wish more than anything that you and Ben went to the same school. To have him in the same building—to see him at your locker in between classes—would give you the confidence you need to get through the day. You're so not in the mood to watch the Instagrammers pose with one another on the first day of school as they snap their pictures and post them, then watch as they slink their way through the halls. You're not in the mood to listen to their chatter about what they did all summer long, to watch as they flit from group to group, making their way through the crowds of popular people, flipping their hair, flaunting their bodies as if they were the most important people on earth.

You get downstairs and Todd has already left in his car for football practice. You don't understand why a team needs to practice twice a day but when you say anything about this to Todd, he simply says, "State champs two years in a row, sis."

Although you can't stand Todd, you wish you didn't have to take the school bus, but getting out the door at six a.m. is not really something you want to do. And Jae lives in the other direction from school so she can't pick you up, so the bus it is.

Your mom asks what you would like for breakfast but you don't feel like you can eat. Still she makes you drink a Carnation Instant milk and the monster quits scratching, just long enough for you to grab your bag and head to the bus.

You sit by yourself, lean against the cool glass of the window, and put your earbuds in. You check your phone and there's a text from Jae:

See you at lunch?

Okay

It's enough to give you a little bit of the courage that you need. Then a text from Ben comes in.

Hey

Instantly, you feel better. Like the monster might lie down and at least sleep for a while.

Hey back

Thinking of you

Me too. I'm on the bus

Sounds fun

Not

Text you when I can today

Ok

XO

He's never XO'ed you before and this makes you extremely happy. This might get you through the day. But still, you're worried about things. Ben doesn't know how hard school is going to be for you. You haven't told him about Alex and the breakup last year, and the not eating and the fainting and the hospital trip. And the rumors.

Ben knows about the food stuff now—the ARFID—but not the stuff that scares you. Your list of fears. The monster. You're so afraid to tell him everything because you don't want to lose him. Your biggest fear. You don't want to tell Ben because you're falling too in love with him and if he discovers this about you—all this stuff you're scared of, the monster that holes up inside you, controls you—well then, maybe Ben won't feel the same way about you as he does now.

So you've kept quiet about the things that terrify you. You think that through therapy, and by trying to be brave, you can kick this on your own, and maybe you won't have to tell him. You're desperately trying to kill the monster on your own, not knowing that you'll need an army.

25

School is slow agony.

The teachers drone on and on about curriculum and go over the syllabi and class requirements. You listen half to them and half to the monster telling you that you can't do this, you can't make it through the day. You're anxious, unsure of yourself, and you don't feel a connection with any of your teachers.

And you're hungry.

It's been a long morning and you haven't eaten anything. During the summer, food was always available when you needed to eat—you could stop by the pantry and get a couple of crackers to quiet the monster. Or grab a handful of potato chips. To shut the bastard up. Now you can't eat anytime you want because you're in classes all morning, and the monster is angry-growling.

You're very cranky.

Right before lunch you walk into your English class and there he is, Alex. You knew you'd see him eventually, but you had no idea he would end up in one of your classes.

You freeze at the doorway; it's the fight-or-flight feeling, and your adrenaline flows through your veins, ice-cold. You want to flee so badly, but you can't. He's sitting on top of one of the desks, talking to a popular girl, the one who has two-hundred-thousand-plus Instagram followers. But. When he sees you in the doorway, he stops talking and stares at you. He's just looking at you. And you do not move.

Until someone shoves past you and knocks into your shoulder and then you move through the doorway to find a seat in the middle-back of the room.

Alex.

He watches you. Eyes on you the whole time.

You hate him. He must know you hate him. Yet he was staring at you.

Why was he staring at you?

He takes a seat two rows behind the Instagrammer girl, which is one row behind where you are sitting, and two seats over. He's got a perfect view of you.

He's looking at you, still staring, you can feel it. You take your notebook, grab a pen, uncap it, and start writing.

Fuck you, Alex is what comes out of your pen and onto the paper.

At lunch, you meet up with Jae, who has her friend Mandi with her, and the three of you find a place to eat in the cafeteria. Your mom packed a lunch she knew you could eat: a mini-bagel with peanut butter, pretzels, a few carrots, and a small baggie of popcorn. Jae and Mandi have bagged lunches too, and they unpack their food. As you're all eating, you discuss how your morning classes went. When you tell Jae you have a class with Alex she says she has one with him too.

"He asked about you," she adds.

"What?"

"Yep, he asked if you were dating anyone."

You shake your head in disbelief.

Mandi chimes in, "He did. I'm in Chemistry with them too."

"Are you freaking kidding me? After last year? What did you tell him?"

"I said he'd have to ask you."

"Why'd you tell him *that*? I don't want to talk to him!" you say.

"Whatever," Jae says, and takes a bite of her sandwich. "You'll probably have to talk to him if you have class with him."

"I'm never going to talk to him." You have finished your bagel and are halfway through your popcorn.

"Well, good luck with that," Mandi says.

You hate the fact that Alex is asking about you. You hated that he stared at you in English class. You don't want to see him every day. You don't want to think about him. Ever. But now you'll have to. You don't want him around, but when you go to your last period, Alex is there too, in your Spanish class.

This time he takes a seat right next to you. You do your best to ignore him but since this is Spanish II, your teacher suggests you turn to the person next to you and introduce yourself. In Spanish.

Alex turns to you and tells you his name in Spanish. You stare at him. The monster is fired up.

"Aren't you going to talk to me?" he asks.

"Not really."

"You have to."

"You were pretty shitty to me last year. Like real shitty."

"I know," he says. "I'm sorry."

"It's way too late for that."

"I was hoping we could talk."

The teacher sees you two are talking, and that it's not in Spanish.

"Señor! Señorita! Problemas?"

"No hay problema. Lo siento," you say. You put your head on your desk.

You knew today was going to be bad but you didn't think it was going to be horrible.

You sense the monster growing.

26

Ben has to watch his little sisters while his parents go to a wedding and he invites you to hang out with them. He picks you up and takes you over to his house, where you greet Earl in the hallway. Ben's parents are on their way out and Dan laughs when he sees you.

"So Ben can't handle the girls on his own?" Dan asks.

"Dad!" Ben says. "You know they're little devils. I needed some backup!"

"Not a problem," Dan says.

Mrs. Hansworth says, "We left money on the counter so you can get ice cream later."

"Thanks. Is that what they're eating for dinner?" Ben asks.

His mom rolls her eyes. "Frozen pizza's fine," she says. "Figure it out, you're seventeen."

"Okay, well you better get out of here then, you don't want to miss those wedding vows!" Ben says.

"Ben can drive you home when we get back. I know the girls

were looking forward to you coming," Mrs. Hansworth says to you. "You have fun, and make sure the girls behave!"

"They will," Ben says as his parents leave.

"Bye," you say to them.

Alana and Olivia tumble down the stairs in fits of giggles. "Did somebody say ice cream?" You know for sure it was Alana, because she's got the shorter hair. The twins climb on Ben and tackle him to the ground. "Ice cream! Ice cream! We want ice cream now!"

Ben lets them attack him and you wonder what it would be like to have a good relationship with Todd, to have ever been playful with him. It makes you sad and wistful to see Ben and his sisters like this.

Ben looks up from where he's being attacked on the floor. "You going to just stand there or you going to help your boyfriend?"

So you jump onto the pile and start tickling.

After frozen pizza (where you try your best but end up scraping the cheese off) and a trip to Dairy Bliss, you get back to Ben's house and the girls ask what you can do next. Ben looks to you for a suggestion.

"You girls want to draw?" you ask.

"Yeah! Let's draw something!" Olivia shouts.

The girls run to get art supplies and Ben asks if you're really up for that because it's getting late.

"Sure, it'll be fun. Plus, I told you I would sketch you sometime, so why not now?"

"Oh great," Ben says. "I can only imagine what you can create with a bunch of crayons and Sharpies."

The girls toss a packet of plain paper and a shoebox filled with markers, pens, pencils, and crayons onto the kitchen table. You rummage through the box, searching for the pens and markers you want to work with.

"Okay," you say to Alana and Olivia. "We're all going to draw what we think Ben looks like to us!"

Alana and Olivia immediately crack up. "This is going to be so much fun!" Alana says.

"I have a great idea!" says Olivia, and they both grab their paper and begin to work.

Ben heads to the refrigerator but you stop him. "Get back here. I need to look at you."

"I'm just getting something to drink. I have a feeling this is going to take a while."

Ben comes back to the table with two bottled waters and sits in the chair next to you. You grab his chin and hold it still for a moment. And then you move closer to him and stare.

You rub your thumb along his jawline, feel the stubble on his face, and smooth your fingers along the edge of his cheekbones.

The girls are scritch-scratching away on their paper, mumbling things about Ben looking like a "big ole monkey," but you are mesmerized by his eyes, his nose, his strong jaw, the curve of his ears. It's like it's just the two of you in the room, and you're holding his face in place, studying him, and he reaches his hand up to circle your wrist and he whispers your name in an achy, painful way.

"Eww! They're gonna kiss!"

You're not sure which twin said it but the spell is broken.

"Okay, bedtime!" Ben says.

"But we're not done!" Alana says.

"Ten more minutes, then upstairs to wash up and brush your teeth and get into your pajamas."

He smiles at you, and you want to melt. He reaches for your thigh under the table and gives it a squeeze. Your desire for this boy grows.

The girls ask your advice on their pictures—*"Should Ben's monkey nose be bigger?"* and *"How about these hairy feet?"*—and then they are done with their pictures and hang their masterpieces on the fridge.

"When are you going to start yours?" Olivia asks you.

"I'll start while you girls are getting ready for bed. I had to think about it first, but it'll be here in the morning, so you can see it then."

Ben takes the girls upstairs and you grab a pencil and a thin black Sharpie and get to work.

Twenty minutes later, as you're putting the finishing touches on your sketch, Ben calls for you to come upstairs to help tuck the girls into their beds.

"Ooh, I like your jammies!" you tell them when you get to their room.

"Thanks, they're paisley print!" Olivia says.

"I know." You laugh.

"That means intricate," Alana says.

"And beautiful!" Olivia adds.

"I'd agree," Ben says. He hugs you close to him.

"You two should totally get married," Olivia exclaims.

"Yes!" Alana shouts from her bed.

"And why is that?" Ben asks, smirking at you.

"Because . . . just . . . it would be fun!" Alana giggles.

"Yes, and then we'd have a big sister!" Olivia adds.

"You two are goofballs," you tell them, pulling blankets up to their necks.

"Is that good or bad?" Alana asks.

"That's wonderful!" you say. "You guys are my most favorite goofballs I've ever known!"

"Well, then, you're my favoritest goofball too!" Alana says.

"Mine too! I want you to be my favoritest goofball too!" Olivia adds.

"Okay, all three of you are goofballs, and I'm taking *this* goofball out of here now, so you two goofballs can get some sleep, all right?" Ben says.

"Ben can't be a goofball because he's a doofus!" Alana says.

"Good night," Ben says.

"Night, girls," you say.

"Wait! Did you finish your picture of Ben?" Olivia asks.

"Yes. You can see it in the morning. Good night."

"Keep the hall light on!" one of the twins says as you head into the hallway.

Ben says, "I will, but only if you keep quiet and go to sleep. Promise."

"Promise!" they both chime.

"God," Ben whispers to you as you both head down the stairs. "That was rough."

"It was fun," you say.

"You *are* a goofball," he says.

In the kitchen you give him your drawing. You drew it fast, but you can tell Ben's impressed.

"Wow. It looks just like me. That's amazing."

"Thanks." You feel a little shy from his compliment.

"It's beautiful. I love it." Ben takes your hand, tilts his head, and says, "Come on."

It's dark in the family room except for the soft glow from the upstairs hall light Ben left on. He leads you to the couch and lays you down and then lies next to you. Neither of you says anything for a long while. He just plays with your hair, touches your face, and looks into your eyes. The house is quiet except for the ticking of the kitchen clock, the hum of the air conditioner, and the sound of your heart beating from within. You can hear that. That's loud and clear.

You lie like that for a very long time, and then he nuzzles his head into your neck and inhales. He says your name.

"I love spending time with you," he says. "I love being with you. I love everything about you."

"Why?"

You're not fishing for compliments, but you really want to know. Because so often you don't feel like you're anything that special or important.

Ben's quiet for a moment and you're glad the room is dark, then he speaks.

"Well," he says, "for one, you have a good heart, and you're sensitive. You're not like other girls who only care about themselves, the way they look, or how others perceive them.

"I watch you with my sisters and they already adore you. I mean, you hardly know them and you're so sweet to them. Two, you make me laugh, I have fun with you. I *think* you have fun with me. I think we get along really well." And this is where he stops and kisses you on the bridge of your nose. "You need more?" he asks. "Because I could continue."

"No, I'm good," you say. You reach up and run your fingers through his hair, remembering what it was like the first time you saw him on the river, how your breath caught at the sight of him. "Thanks."

"For what?" Ben asks.

"For making me so happy."

And then you take advantage of the quiet of the house, the darkness surrounding you, the fact that you and Ben are alone on the couch snuggling, and you kiss him.

27

You've heard therapy starts out easy and then gets worse, and you're seeing firsthand that it's true. In one-on-one with Shayna, it's mostly been discussion, but today she's starting sensory therapy, where she is reintroducing foods to you.

She has brought in a bunch of foods she wants you to describe, including some safe foods. You'll tell her your anxiety level with each item, what they look like to you, how they feel, which ones smell good, and which ones smell bad.

She shows you mushrooms, chives, beef jerky, eggplant, pineapple, carrots, beets, apples, cabbage, plums, garlic—and other things that you've only ever seen at the grocery store, things you've never imagined touching or tasting—and asks you to organize them from prettiest to ugliest, and then from best-smelling to worst. Some of it is fun, because some of the things are beautiful, like the smooth, shiny purple-black eggplant whose skin you can practically see your reflection in. Or the prickly pineapple: when you sniff at the bottom, you imagine a tropical island. Those are interesting foods that you have never considered touching or smelling.

Those things are easy for you to do. Because you aren't tasting the foods. You are just looking, smelling, and touching. That feels safe.

But when Shayna asks you to think about smell and taste together, and to describe that, your brain can't work that way. You actually like the smell of beef jerky but the idea of putting it into your mouth, of chewing something that is probably thick like a cord, and rubbery . . . You can't imagine what that would be like. The thought of eating something as repulsive as beef jerky brings you no comfort. You see no point in putting something that unappealing into your mouth and chewing until you could finally get it down your throat to feed the monster. And you aren't going to do that.

"I'm not asking you to chew and swallow foods today, unless you feel like you want to?" Shayna says. "If you want to try something, you're welcome to taste. Maybe put a piece of something into your mouth and see what happens. See if something might surprise you?" she suggests.

It's the first therapy session since school has started and you're stressed. You tell Shayna you're not ready, that you can't focus on this stuff.

"School has been awful. I didn't expect Alex to be in two of my classes."

Shayna knows all about Alex and your hospital trip last year, so she understands your anxiety.

"Tell me what you're feeling," she says.

You don't want to talk about this with Shayna right now—it's been hard enough seeing Alex in English and Spanish every day. But talking about Alex is better than thinking about how beef jerky and plums might taste rolling around the inside of your mouth.

Still, you don't say anything immediately.

Shayna nudges you on. "Want to talk about the breakup?"

You think about it.

Then you answer her question.

"I think it was all my fault. I couldn't do the things a regular girlfriend could do," you finally say.

"Why not?"

You break down. You know why. Shayna knows why too. It was because you weren't normal. You aren't normal.

"I couldn't go out to dinners, or go to parties. I couldn't *be* social. So it was pretty much all my fault that he broke up with me." You wipe tears from your eyes.

It might not seem like a big deal to regular people. But you know how it feels, and when you can't eat a normal meal, when you are scared of trying new things, and you feel like you can't be social because there's food involved, it suffocates you. You know this now. And you also know you can't live this way anymore.

But you also know you don't feel anywhere near ready to try the foods that Shayna has placed before you.

"And I can't eat this stuff you want me to eat—obviously not today—and I don't know when I might be able to. Shit, I can't even eat a regular piece of pizza with cheese with Ben. I have to take the cheese off it."

You're still crying, hard, desperate tears, and Shayna watches you, lets you cry. Because that's part of her job, to let you get the tears out. Then she hands you a box of tissues, letting you know the cryfest is just about over.

You take the tissues and blow your nose.

"I don't know if I can do this."

"Do what?" Shayna asks.

"I don't think I can get better."

Shayna says nothing, which is another thing you've learned that therapists do: they don't have to say a lot and they get paid a ton of money. She'll sit and wait until you feel like talking more.

"It's like, I want to get better, but I'm afraid."

Nod.

"I feel like I don't know how to get better. I don't want to eat these foods you're showing me. Like ever."

Another nod.

"I feel like these foods aren't going to cure me. How is eating a mushroom going to make me more social?"

Another nod.

"And this has nothing to do with food, but I'm so stressed. School is hard. Therapy is hard. My parents stress me out."

"The stress and anxiety you're experiencing have everything to do with having ARFID. When you learn to eat, even if it's just a few new foods, you'll be more comfortable, and you'll become more social, which will alleviate stress and anxiety."

You think about this, then you switch gears. "The only thing I have going for me is Ben and since school started I've only seen him once."

You realize that sounds tragic, like a Romeo and Juliet saga, but still, you're afraid that you're not going to see Ben as much as you want to, and he's the only one who keeps you sane. He's the only one who seems to keep the monster at a lull.

28

How about I pick you up after school?

It's Wednesday morning and you're on the bus and you feel your whole face light up when you read the text from Ben.

Of course!

OK, 2:30 by the front doors?

Sounds good.

See you then XO

XO ☺

This is the first time you've XO'ed him back and it definitely feels like a shift in your relationship. You're absolutely giddy over this and you've never had a better day at school. Sure, you've only been in school for a week but all you think about is how your boyfriend is coming to get you after school. You completely ignore Alex's stares in English and in Spanish and the day goes by surprisingly fast.

At two-twenty, you say goodbye to Jae and make your way to the front of the school. As you wait, you busy yourself checking out the latest from the infamous Instagrammers. Yep, they're still there, posting selfies in sports bras and Nike work-out shorts, looking slutty as usual. You wonder if their moms have any clue about the pictures they post and the comments they get.

Next, you check Todd's Twitter feed to see what he's been up to because that's the only connection you have to your brother and his life. You see he's really pumped for Friday night's football game and he's encouraging everyone to go support the team. He's got seventy-six retweets.

You check the time on your phone and wonder where Ben is. There's no text from him and you start to worry because it's two-forty-five now and practically everyone is gone from school. Only you and a couple of other kids are waiting for rides. You text Ben:

You almost here?

When there is no answer by three o'clock you become fran-tic, thinking he's been in a car accident and he's dead. Just what you need: a dead boyfriend you haven't even had the chance to tell that you love. A couple of kids on skateboards whiz by, nearly taking you out, and they say, "Whoa, sorry dude," as they continue past. You're near tears by this point, sure that Ben is dead.

At three-ten you get a text:

Got caught up but I'm on my way!

Through tears you send him a text that you're already home,

saying you got a ride with Todd. Now you wish he *was* dead, because you want to kill him.

You walk to the football field where Todd is practicing with the team. The aluminum bleachers are so hot you burn the backs of your thighs when you sit. You don't want to wait for Todd but you don't have any other way home and you don't want to call your mom. The sun beats down on you so hard you feel dizzy, and beads of sweat form on your upper lip, but you wait.

When the football coach blows his whistle signaling practice is over, you walk toward the turf and the players, and your brother catches your eye.

"What's up?" he asks.

"Can I get a ride?"

"Sure," he says, as he pulls his helmet from his sweaty head. He smells like dirt and stink and it's weird because this is your brother but you hardly know him. You both walk in silence to the parking lot where he gets into the car and unlocks it for you from the inside.

Instead of putting on the air conditioner, Todd rolls down the front windows and sticks his forearm out of the car. It's too hot for the car windows to be open, and the stench of him is repulsive but you can't complain because he's giving you a ride home. You swallow down the bile that's building in your throat.

"Did you miss the bus or just want to watch me in action?" he asks.

"Ben was supposed to pick me up."

"He blew you off? Knew he was a dick."

You turn your head toward your open window and say nothing more.

You go straight to your room. Ben has let you down. He offered to do something nice for you, and then he let you down. And thought nothing of it. He got "caught up" but was on his way? You're that important to him and that's all he could say? No *I'm sorry I'm late*? You're so upset.

All evening you hear texts and calls coming through, but you don't look at your phone. The monster is fuming. Sometimes you can't tell if it's you or the monster who's angry, or if you're fusing into the same being. It's becoming more and more difficult. One minute, you're the happiest you've ever felt—when Ben texted you that morning, offering to get you after school—and now? Now you feel so let down.

You want to quit everything.

You shut off your phone for the night and you and your monster go to sleep.

29

At lunch the next day you tell Jae and Mandi what happened.

"Ben totally blew me off after telling me he would pick me up. I thought he was dead and when he said he was on his way, it was like no big deal that he was almost forty-five minutes late. Like he didn't even care that I waited for him for so long."

"There's got to be a valid reason. He wouldn't purposely make you wait," Jae says. "You're being ridiculous."

"Yeah, you really are being crazy over this," Mandi says.

It's totally okay for Jae to tell you that you're being ridiculous, but when Mandi calls you crazy, you glare at her. She hardly knows you, so who's she to say if you're crazy or not, although you think you *are* crazy these days.

"What'd he say today?" Jae asks as she takes a bite of a meaty sandwich that makes you want to barf.

"I don't know. I haven't turned my phone back on."

"Do you or do you not want to be with him?" Jae asks.

You sigh, a deep, heavy, sad sigh. "I do. So badly."

"Give me the damn phone." Jae holds out her hand.

You give her the phone, afraid of what she's going to find. When she turns it on, it almost sounds as if it's exploding because there are so many chimes going off–beep after beep after beep, and you're sure they're all from Ben.

"Twenty-six messages, you idiot. Twenty-six."

Jae starts typing immediately.

"What are you doing?!" you yell.

"Fixing this." Jae sends a message and in a matter of seconds there's a response. She texts back and forth a few times with Ben and when she's done, she tells you, "I told Ben it was me texting from your phone. He had to stay after school yesterday because the track coach wanted to talk to him. He said he tried to tell you that yesterday, but you didn't read his texts or answer his calls."

You don't know what to say.

"He's going to meet you out front after school," Jae says, and then: "You better not blow this with him. You should have let him explain and apologize. You owe him an apology too."

You thank Jae and tell her you're sorry for being so stupid.

"Tell him that," she says.

After school, you head out the main doors and Ben's waiting for you, holding a bouquet of baby-white carnations. You walk over to him, feeling shy and embarrassed about your behavior.

When you reach him, you both start to say something, so then you laugh and he hands you the flowers.

"Someone told me these are your favorite," he says.

"Red roses are so cliché," you say.

"Come here." He pulls you in for a hug. While you're not looking at him it feels easier and you try it again.

"I'm sorry," you say.

"I'm sorry too," he says, still hugging you.

"You don't need to apologize," you say. "I was an ass. But I thought you were dead. I was so worried. And then I got mad at you. I'm sorry I was such a bitch and didn't give you a chance to explain."

You don't want to let go of him so you keep hugging Ben, right at the front of your school. You can't believe you almost screwed it up over something so stupid. You're so stupid.

"We okay?" he asks.

"We're okay," you say. You so want to believe it.

30

It's Saturday night. Your parents are out, and Todd is in his room, probably plugged into his earbuds. Ben is over. You're feeling inklings of the monster lurking; he's getting in the way tonight, telling you that you're not good enough for Ben, that someone like Ben will never love you, that you're not good enough for anyone. Your anxiety is rising and usually when you're with Ben it's lowered. This is not normal and you're quiet.

You're sullen. You're moody.

Ben can tell.

You're on the couch, trying to watch TV, but the monster is vying for your attention. It's like you, Ben, and the monster. Like the monster is third-wheeling. You click the remote control to turn off the TV.

"What's the matter?" Ben has his arm around you, then he takes your hand in his. The monster howls as if Ben's touch burns him.

"I don't feel very well?" you say.

"You hungry?" Ben asks, and he pulls you up from the couch. "Let's get something to eat." You don't want to eat, but Ben is dragging you into the kitchen.

Ben opens the fridge and looks around, rummaging through Tupperware and tin-foiled leftovers, stuff you know you will not touch. It bothers you that Ben is going through your refrigerator.

"What do you have in here?" he asks.

"Like I know." It comes out very rude.

"Don't be like that," he says.

"I'm not hungry," you say.

"You should eat something. What did you eat today?"

"Stop."

He turns his head from the fridge and looks at you.

It was the monster that said *stop*. Not you. You're sure of it. Because it came out mean and sharp, not how you talk to Ben.

"What? Why?" he asks kindly.

"Don't be my therapist. I don't want to eat," you say. Again, the monster.

He closes the fridge. Looks at you.

"Are you okay?" he asks.

Your bottom lip is quivering. You don't know what to say. On the one hand you want to cry, you want to fall into his arms and admit you need help, more help than you're getting. Maybe you shouldn't have stopped taking your pills. Maybe it was a dumb idea to think you were getting better on your own?

You can't go on like this, you don't feel strong enough, and you wish you could tell Ben that you aren't sure what's happening, but that you're extremely sad, and you don't know what's going on inside you.

But. You know it's the monster and you can't control it when things like this happen. Because if you could control anything, you'd be able to get rid of the monster. And he's still there.

You pull yourself together and your lip stops quivering.

Ben is still looking at you. You can tell he's hurt by your attitude, but there's nothing you can do about it because the monster's got full control. This is exactly what you've been afraid of. Because of this disorder, and because of this monster, you're pushing away the people you love. It's happening with Ben.

"Maybe you should just go home."

"You really want me to go home?" he asks, hurt.

"I just don't feel well, and I think I should go to bed before I do something not right."

"What do you mean?" he asks.

"I don't know."

"Are you okay?" he asks again.

"I need to be alone."

"I don't think you should be alone." He sounds demanding to you. The monster tells you that Ben is bossing you around. The monster tells you that Ben is complicating your life, and he doesn't care for you, only the monster cares for you. This boy, who you've known for only six weeks, is using you. The monster says that this boy, this boy in your house now, who's telling you what to do, is not important, and the monster knows what's best for you, because he's been there with you from the beginning.

So the monster tells you what to say next.

"Just go."

"You sure?" He's giving you another chance.

Take it, you think.

The monster says no.

"I'm sure."

"Okay."

And Ben leaves.

31

It's the Monday after you made Ben leave and you don't know how you managed to get through school. You lied to Jae and told her you had to work on math homework during lunch so you didn't have to see her and you went to the library instead. She would know immediately that something was seriously wrong; she'd see it on your face and she'd know right away. And you can't face her.

After school your mom comes up to your room to get you for therapy. You tell her you're not up for it.

"You can't skip it. We'll be charged ninety dollars for missing a session. And besides, you're doing really well. I think you're getting better."

"Mom, it's not helping. None of it is. I can't do it. Shayna wants me to start tasting foods soon and–"

Your mom cuts you off. "I'm not arguing with you on this one. You're going. You need to go."

She has no clue. But you don't have a say in the matter and

she takes you to therapy. Fortunately, Shayna has decided to take a break and skip the food part this week because it stressed you out so much last week. Instead, she does some touch therapy on you where you don't have to talk that much. You're so glad because if she asks you about Ben you're sure you'll burst into tears.

Later, during group, you sit with the other girls—the ones who don't eat and the ones who throw up—and you are quiet as you listen to everyone talk about how they are either struggling to eat a salad or struggling not to puke, and you want to die.

You don't want to be here.

After a while, Shayna notices you are not saying anything, so she puts you on the spot and asks if you have anything to add.

You stay silent for a while, and it's the uncomfortable type of silence where everyone is staring at you, waiting for you to say something, and you don't really want to talk but then you just spill out the words. Mostly because you want to know if you're the only one.

"Do any of you have monsters inside of you?"

When no one says anything you keep talking.

"Because I have a monster. I have a monster that lives in me. This monster, sometimes he's noisy and sometimes he's not so loud, but he's always here, and he's always, always telling me what to do. He's responsible for my food problems—making it impossible to eat or try new things. He also makes me anxious and depressed and sad because he tells me what I should think, what I should say, what I should do. And then I do it. No matter what it is. And sometimes I do horrible things."

You don't tell them what you did after Ben left Saturday night. You can't. The monster won't let you. You'll get in trouble. You feel your nose get tickly and you are pretty sure you're going to cry but then your monster tells you not to be a baby, not to cry, so you don't. Because you always listen to the monster.

"The other night, I made my boyfriend leave because of the monster, and he wasn't doing anything wrong. And I didn't want him to leave and now I think we broke up. This monster makes me do bad things. Do you guys have any idea what I'm talking about?"

"You mean like Ed?" one of the girls asks.

Shayna interrupts. "*Ed* is a term we use for *eating disorder*, like we've given it an identity."

You look at Shayna and then address the girls again. "It's worse than Ed. It's like having Ed plus having a real monster. One who controls every part of your existence. Like for-real real. Like I wake up every single day hoping the monster is dead but he's not. He's not dead. He's not leaving. I can't get him to leave."

One of the girls—Nina, she's textbook anorexic—comes over and hugs you. She's standing and you're still sitting and it's a totally awkward hug, because she's much too thin and has sharp elbow edges, plus you don't even know her. You don't hug her back, but that doesn't stop her from hugging you harder. This is extremely annoying to you, and then Hailey gets up and group-hugs you.

Jesus Christ, you think.

"I'm so sorry you're going through this," Nina says.

"I hate the fucking monster," you say. "I need it to die."

Nina pats you on the head and says, "I know, I know." Her breath stinks. You imagine it's what death smells like.

You try to pull away. "Please stop hugging me."

32

It started the night Ben left your house. And every day it gets worse.

The strange thing, the craziest thing about it, is you watch in amazement and can't believe you can't feel it.

You can't *feel* any of it.

That's not exactly true. You do feel something.

You feel calm.

The first time you were in the kitchen. Right after you made Ben leave that night, you sat at the kitchen counter, humming to yourself. Although you couldn't tell if it was you humming, or if the monster was humming. You felt a buzzing, vibrating sound coming from inside. It was echoing and it felt like a force from within. There had been a safety pin on the counter.

A random safety pin.

You picked it up and unlatched it and at first you touched the sharp edge to your thumbnail. You pushed back your cuticle and picked at the skin with the pin. You felt like you might cry because you had made Ben leave, but you forced yourself not to shed tears. It wasn't you who wanted Ben to go. The monster wanted him to leave. And so he left.

He was gone.

And you were alone.

Alone with the monster.

You pushed your cuticle back on your thumb and then you went through all your nails. All ten of them: you pushed your cuticles back and thought about what you had done. You were mean to Ben and you told him to leave. He left. You should have gone after him and told him you were sorry, explained to him that you hadn't meant to be rude, that you were out of sorts, not yourself, and you didn't really want him to leave.

You should have done the simple thing, the right thing, and apologized.

But the monster told you no. Told you to stay there.

So you did.

You had taken the safety pin and pressed your cuticles back with the sharp point, testing the soft area of your skin, and then you scraped them down some more, slowly and deliberately, until they turned pink. Then you scraped until blood came. But you didn't feel anything like hurt. Nothing. Six of your nail beds bled.

You thought you should have felt something but you didn't. You heard the humming still, but it didn't bother you, it just encouraged you. You kept scraping and scraping until more blood pooled from your nail beds, and then you got tired of it so you took the pin and put it down on the counter.

You looked at your left thumbprint, the tiny circles looping round and round, and you noticed lines intersecting the circles; you had never looked that close before. You picked up the safety pin again, traced across those horizontal lines on your thumb, and jabbed at your thumbprint, tried to scrape it from your thumb. You scratched furiously at it, wanting to erase it. It didn't go anywhere.

The humming, you almost could recognize the tune; not quite, but it was still there, in your ears, like a soft rain, lulling you into a trance. It was comforting.

When you got bored, you went upstairs, knowing that Ben wasn't going to come back, he wasn't going to call or text. It would be up to you to apologize. You were the one who hurt him.

After that night, you keep the safety pin with you. It doesn't hurt when you do it, and it's just a little scraping on skin. You've decided it's a coping skill. Shayna has taught you about coping skills. Like meditation and yoga. Taking walks and listening to relaxing music—soft drums and chants, maybe a river flowing—something to calm you, almost like the humming you do, which sounds like a soft rain. The humming that accompanies the safety-pin activity is soothing.

So the safety pin is a coping skill. It's easy to keep with you, and after all, it's "safe." A "safety" pin. When you feel stressed or unnerved or like the monster is getting too loud, you take the pin and scrape and scratch. At first you focus on your fingernails, and in between your fingers, sometimes on the sides of your wrists, but really, really gently, until the skin turns white and flaky.

You convince yourself this is okay. This is nothing bad. It's not like you're going to kill yourself. This is not a razor or a knife. It's a small safety pin. You only do it for a short while, the scraping, just a few minutes at most. And the blood, when the blood finally comes, doesn't spurt out, and sometimes there's no blood at all. But when it comes, it's subtle, like a soft ooze, so subtle that no one knows. No one but you and the monster. It's not hard to hide it from your parents either. You camp out in your room, avoid dinners, the usual. They leave you alone and when your mom does check on you, you tell her you're doing homework.

The times when you get out the safety pin and scrape—when you see that crimson red skim the surface of your skin—you feel relief from some of the internal pain you're feeling. It's almost like letting out a little bit of air from a balloon that's been blown up too much. You just need to let some of that air out so you can breathe.

That's all.

That's all this is, you're sure. You're letting the monster breathe a bit. And when some of the blood comes, it's like you're giving him air.

He's quiet. And you're calm.

33

Alex continues to watch you in school and you continue to ignore him. He's tried to talk to you a few times but you want nothing to do with him. The rumor mill has been quiet and you know that if there's any communication between the two of you, you run the risk of rumors resurfacing. And you don't need that drama. You're barely getting through your days at school as it is, and since you haven't talked to Ben, you can hardly concentrate.

You do your best to focus on getting through one class at a time.

Just get through one class at a time, that's all you think when you're at school.

On Thursday, in English, Mr. Owens assigns the first of what he says will be many in-class assignments.

"As juniors, you're going to be doing a lot of writing in here, but to get started, I want to begin with something simple. We'll work it into an essay later in the semester," he says, rocking on his heels.

You wish Mr. Owens wouldn't rock on his heels because it looks like he's about to fall over at any minute.

You wish Alex wasn't in this class with you.

You wish you could go back to Saturday night and have a do-over with Ben.

You also wish you didn't have to bring the monster to school because you think you might have really enjoyed this class. You used to love English.

You used to love a lot of things.

Now you can't think of a thing you love.

Except for Ben.

You were beginning to love Ben. But you told him to go away. Apparently, he is a very good listener.

You feel the urge take claim so you unhook the safety pin from the inside of your T-shirt where you've pinned it.

The internal humming begins. Because you can't hum out loud here, the monster does it for you.

Your aim is the inside edge of your left wrist, just below the sleeve of the flannel you wore over your T-shirt. Your hands are tucked between your thighs, under your desk, and with the precision of a surgeon you hold the safety pin between your thumb and forefinger and scrape lightly. You've been doing this for less than a week but already you have a system figured out, a way to do this in class so no one knows.

You wish you could tell Shayna or Jae how it makes you feel, how it shuts the monster up, but you can't tell anyone. It is almost like a drug and you can't explain it because if you told anyone, they'd think you were crazy.

But maybe.

Maybe you are crazy.

Because.

You don't eat.

There's a monster living inside you.

The boy you thought you were falling in love with is now gone.

School sucks.

Your ex-boyfriend watches you all the time.

You're coping by scratching at your skin with a safety pin.

Your name is called and you see Mr. Owens staring at you.

"Did you get all that?" he asks.

"Yep," you say with surprising fake confidence.

"Great, so, the assignment, due at the end of class."

Everyone shuffles in their seats and grabs pens and sheets of paper from their binders to begin their work. The girl next to you knows you have no clue what you're supposed to do. She places a blank sheet of lined paper on your desk and whispers, "Six-word memoir about you. Your life."

"Thanks, thanks so much," you whisper back gratefully.

A six-word memoir. *So easy,* you think, as you jot down the first thing that comes to mind:

The monster inside wants me dead.

Then you go back to your scraping while the rest of the class continues to think about their lives in six words.

You're in a zone, silently scraping away, when the girl who gave you the paper taps you on the shoulder and whispers, "What are you doing?"

You quickly move your right hand away to hide the pin, but you're sure she saw. And then you see the blood. It's not anything to be freaked out by, but a little line of red has bubbled up and rivers down the palm of your hand. While it doesn't seem like a big deal, this would get a whole lot of people talking if it got around.

"Christ." You don't have anything to clean it up with so you pull your sleeve over your hand and make a fist. You collect your things and head to Mr. Owens's desk.

"Mr. Owens, can I go to the nurse?" you ask.

"What's the matter?" He doesn't see the blood.

You give him the answer that will get any girl out of a classroom fast. "My period."

"Go."

"Thank you."

You put your assignment in Mr. Owens's in-box before you leave.

At the nurse's office, you tell her that you have bad cramps and ask if she can call your mom to pick you up.

Your mom picks you up from school and when you get home you go to your room and continue to scrape until more blood oozes out.

Then you feel the calm you were waiting for.

34

The next morning you don't get up for school. You can't. The monster makes you sleep. Your mom tries to get you up.

"Can't. Cramps are still bad. And head kills," you say from under your covers. You make sure your wrists are hidden from her. They are red and raw.

She closes the door and you go back to sleep. You sleep all day.

When you wake up you feel a gnawing in your stomach. You know it's a deep hunger, you've felt this way before. And it's an odd thing–to feel hunger but not to desire food. You know your body needs fuel but you have no idea what you'd be able to put into your mouth and chew. You don't know what to feed the monster, what would satiate the emptiness in your stomach, what would fill that hole in you.

You sit up in bed. It's four p.m.

You haven't eaten since breakfast yesterday morning.

You pick up your phone to text Jae, knowing she's got to be pissed at you. At the beginning of the week you'd ditched her by hiding out in the library and you haven't responded to her texts. You're sure she's probably also worried about you.

Hey

Hi

You mad at me?

I'll get over it. Why weren't you at school? What's wrong?

I think Ben and I are over

What? WHY!?

You love Jae so much for this. Because although she may be mad at you, she's still your best friend and she cares about you.

I screwed everything up. I made him leave my house Saturday night.

Oh

Yeah. I don't know WTF I'm doing

You OK?

I honestly don't know

I'm sorry

I'm sorry too. I'm not a very good friend.

I still love you tho

Come over later?

Can't. Gotta pack for the fam Labor Day trip to the lake. We leave in the morning.

Oh forgot! Text me when you get back

K bye

You turn on some music. It's thrashing and loud, music you normally wouldn't choose. It's angsty music. It's good to listen to because you feel angsty. You feel unsettled. How could you have turned Ben away like that, told him to leave, when he was becoming more important to you than anyone, more important than the monster. He could have helped you kill the monster. If only you had told him.

You reach for the safety pins on your nightstand. You have two of them—one small one, and one really big one that could pin together a wool winter coat it's so huge. You take the big one and start scratching at the very center of the inside of your wrist. You scratch and scrape, scrape, scrape. You don't break the skin right at this spot though, because you know.

You know what's underneath that flimsy layer.

It's a blue river vein.

And what's flowing in that river is too important. Maybe.

You're not quite ready for that.

You don't want to give up quite yet.

Sure, you're unhappy. You're so unhappy. The monster's taken everything away from you that you've loved. Your family, your joy, your hope. Ben.

Ben.

The skin at your wrist starts to turn pink, and bits of it flake as you scrape it away and your wrist turns angry. You look at the bulges of blue straining underneath the paper-thin skin. You think it would be so easy, just so very easy to put a little poke there. You wonder what would happen if you just stabbed once.

Twice?

Maybe three quick times?

If you just took the pin to the vein? What could happen? Maybe not much.

Your wrist is really red now, slices of pink etched into your skin, but there's no prickling of blood.

There's a knock on your door. You pull the pin away from your wrist and turn off your music. You slide the pin back onto your nightstand and tuck yourself under your comforter, hiding your wrists.

"Come in."

It's your brother.

Todd never comes to see you.

"What do you want?"

He's got his earbuds around his neck and he sits on the edge of your bed.

"Mom says you're sick."

"Yeah."

"What's the matter?"

"Cramps."

"That sucks," he says.

"I'll be all right. Happens every month."

"Not this bad. You okay?"

You can't believe your brother is actually showing concern for you. This is really strange.

"Do you want something?" you ask.

"Just checking on you."

"I'm fine."

He glances at your nightstand, and you're sure he sees the safety pins but he wouldn't think anything of it. Then he asks, "Where's that guy you've been hanging out with?"

"Not that it's any of your business but I think we broke up."

"Good, I didn't like him."

"God, Todd! You're such an asshole!"

"What? He seemed like a douche. You can do much better."

"You're the douche! Get out of my room."

35

Todd leaves your room and you sink back into your bed, thinking about what a jerk he is. You doze off for a bit and then your mom comes to check on you. What is it with all the sudden concern from everyone? She asks if you've eaten anything. You promise her you'll come down and eat some cereal in a while. You tell her that your cramps are getting better and yes, you *even* smile at her.

She turns to leave your room.

"Close the door please," you ask as nicely as you can.

She goes.

You lie in the quiet and comfort of your room.

You breathe.

You think. About what, you're not sure. But really, you are sure. You know what you're thinking about. It's what you're always thinking about.

Either the monster. Or Ben.

So you text him.

I'm sorry. I'm so sorry.

You need him.

You don't need the monster. You don't need the safety pin.

But maybe you do?

Because after you send the text, you go to work on your right hand—a fresh canvas. But this time you stay away from the rivery veins of the inside of your delicate wrist and move to your palm. You prick at it until you peel away some flesh. You discover a way to take the pin and slip it through the top layer without breaking it, and then you actually close the pin. So the pin is attached to your palm. It looks pretty weird, but cool too. You wonder, if you take five safety pins, could you pin one to each of your fingertips? Could you tap your fingers on the table-top, making music?

Tap, tap, tappity-tap-tap.

At least now you're not wondering what would happen if you let the river of your vein run dry.

You're thinking about all of this when your phone beeps:

Hi

It's Ben.

Your stomach churns and this time it's not from the growling, hungry monster dwelling inside you.

Blood rushes to your head. Before you can think, you text:

Do you hate me?

Of course not

I'm a terrible person

No you're not

I'm so screwed up

I'll give you that ☺

You exhale at the sight of the smiley face. Then you text:

Thank you for texting me back

I was just waiting

you were?

Yeah

I'm really messed up

I don't care

you don't?

No

No?

Nope

So what now?

I see my gf again? And she'll be nice to me?

Yes! Yes! Yes!

36

You know there's no way your parents are going to let you out since you've missed school so you tell Ben to come over at nine o'clock and wait outside for you. He asks if you think that's a good idea and you tell him that it'll be fine.

You go to the kitchen and pour yourself a bowl of cereal—Frosted Flakes—and make small talk with your mom, staying far enough away so she can't see your wrists. You tell her you feel much better and that you're going to go upstairs and try to catch up on some homework.

"That sounds like a good idea. And I'm glad that you're eating something."

You nod and spoon scoops of Frosted Flakes into your mouth. You were so hungry and now the monster has settled. You're not sure if he's quiet because you're eating but you're just glad the monster is not around.

You finish your cereal, put your bowl in the sink, tell your mom you love her, and head toward the stairs. But before you make it up, your dad turns his head from the TV—ESPN is on, of course—and says, "Oh hey, Pea, how you doing?" and then he's right back to *SportsCenter*, not even waiting for your answer. His lack of interest further convinces you that you're leaving the house tonight.

In your room, you text with Jae, tell her you're trying to fix things with Ben. You get out your sketch pad to draw but you can't focus so you put your supplies away. You try to figure out the best way to get out of the house without anyone knowing you're gone. You decide you'll have to sneak out your bedroom window. You've never done anything like this before but you're desperate to see Ben. At eight-thirty you open your bedroom door and yell down to your parents: "I'm really tired, I'm going to bed for the night!"

Both of your parents say good night to you and you hope your mom won't check on you when she goes to bed. You know your dad won't.

At nine o'clock, you climb out your bedroom window and although it must be in the eighties, it feels cool for early September. There's a slow wind and you wonder if maybe there might be one of those last monsoons of the season coming through. You would hate to get caught in a rainstorm on the night you sneak out. Your bedroom is right over the air-conditioning system so it's an easy jump down on top of it. You're worried, though, that when you hit it you'll make too much noise, but since there's no backing out now, you go for it. When you're on the ground, you pause for a moment to see if any out-side lights come on. When they don't, you crouch down and head to the street where Ben is standing outside his car waiting for you.

He's there, waiting.

Ben.

He's smiling.

What you want to do, what you really want to do is fall into his arms and smell him, all of him, and put your fingers through his hair and touch his cheeks and, of course, kiss his lips and also his eyelashes.

But you're tentative and nervous because you were so mean to him the last time he was here.

So instead, you wait and watch. The light from the street lamp hits him just right, so there's a glow about him, and he's got this look on his face, like the first day when you floated on the river together.

You wish you were floating again.

You take a step forward because you figure if you don't do something your knees might give out on you.

He puts both hands out and takes yours in his. His are warm, soft. You've missed his touch more than you knew, and he pulls you to him and touches his thumbs to your wrist, your palms. He feels the rough scrapes you've created there.

He brings you closer, all the while touching your wrists, your fingers and hands, the places you scratched.

He looks into your eyes, and there's such sadness in his expression.

He knows.

He *knows*.

"Oh babe," he says. "What did you do?"

He pulls you closer and you start to cry.

He takes you to his house.

He wanted to take you back into your house, to have you tell your parents right away, to show them what you had done, but you begged him, pleaded with him not to. You said your parents wouldn't understand, that they don't get you and that you can't be near them. So he agreed and he took you to his house.

His sisters are asleep and his parents have gone to their bedroom already so the house is dark when you pull up. Inside, his puppy, Earl, lifts his head from his dog bed and whimpers.

"Not much of a guard dog," Ben jokes.

In the kitchen he turns on the lights.

"Show me," he says.

You're embarrassed. But you trust Ben so you place your hands in his and he carefully examines your palms, your fingertips, your cuticles, and your wrists. He moves his finger across the scratches you've etched into your skin, featherlike. He looks into your eyes as he lifts your hand up to his lips to kiss your fingers.

"Why?" he finally asks.

You thought you'd feel better being with Ben, but you're ashamed. Ashamed that the monster made you do this. You have no answer for Ben when he asks you why. You don't know how to tell him that when you did it you felt relief, and that you only started doing it after he left. You think that would make him feel bad, and you don't want Ben to feel bad. It's not his fault you did this.

You shake your head as if to say *I don't know.*

It's enough for him, because he knows you. Already, in your heart, in his heart, you know each other.

"We can talk about it later."

"Okay," you say.

"You're still perfect," he says.

He takes your hand and leads you to his room. The walls are painted dark blue, and the feeling when you walk in is intense, warm, comforting. A few posters feature some bands you wish you knew all the music of because if it's music he listens to, you're sure you would love it. You imagine him singing to you while you're curled up in his bed. His sheets are a tangled mass, and his comforter—navy and brown—is crumpled at the edge of his bed as if it was too hot and he had to kick it aside. His desk is neat, a stack of notebooks and papers in the corner, his laptop, some pens in a cup. T-shirts are folded on the chair and the only light comes from a small desk lamp.

You sit on the bed, reach for his pillow, and place it on your lap. After a few moments, you bring the pillow up to your face and inhale. It's a real feather pillow, it's cool, and it smells just like Ben. He sits next to you and tells you he missed you.

"I missed you too. I'm sorry."

"Quit saying that," he says.

"But I am."

"I know."

"I'm sorry for everything. I'm not really very good for you."

"Don't say that. But you have to be good for yourself first," he says.

You swallow. You don't want to cry, because you don't want to be sad.

"I wanted to call you, text you, but when you asked me to leave, I figured you didn't want me around," Ben says.

"I know." You swallow again, harder.

"I get that it wasn't you talking that night."

"No."

"Are you on medication?" he asks.

"I was."

"What happened?"

"I stopped taking my antidepressant about three weeks ago."

"Why?"

"Because I thought I was feeling better." Your voice cracks.

"You think you should still take it?" Ben asks.

"Yeah."

"Yeah," he says. "Are you afraid of me?" he wants to know.

"No! Why would you ask me something like that?" you whisper.

"It's just, it seemed like you were pushing me away the other night. I wasn't sure?"

You tell him about Alex, and the rumors from last year, and the ER and how you started taking medication after all that. You tell him how difficult school is. He needs to understand that there are catalysts that have caused you to behave the way you've been acting, and that nothing he's done has made you do what you've done.

"If anything, I'm mostly scared of losing you, that's all. Maybe that's what I'm afraid of," you admit.

"I'm not going anywhere."

He touches your hair, moves it away from your neck, and brings you close to him. You lean along the length of him, put your head on his shoulder. You both sit there for a moment, quietly. You feel a little less sad. You know he cares about you, because he wouldn't say those things if he didn't care, he wouldn't want you here if he didn't care.

He lifts your chin and meets your lips and then you're kissing each other, and you remember how much you love kissing him, and how could you have made him leave your house? Why did you make him go?

The kissing is slow and in between the kisses Ben says your name softly, over and over and over again. You love it when he whispers your name because no one in the world says your name the way he does—it sounds like a light snow falling or rain on a spring day, or dandelions blowing in the wind—all the things you know are beautiful.

He takes the pillow you've been holding and sets it on the floor. He lowers you onto the bed and moves over you, locking one of his legs over one of yours. All the while you keep kissing. Kissing him is that moment between wake and sleep when you're still not sure if you're dreaming.

37

Ben drives you home at eleven-thirty and you sneak in through the garage. There's a light on in the kitchen and you don't think anything of it as you head toward the stairs to your room, but you run right smack into your mother, who's holding a glass of water.

Her eyes bulge out in shock at seeing you there in your regular clothes and your Chucks, and not in your pajamas.

"What in the world? What's going on? Were you out?!"

"Mom!" You think fast. "You scared me! I woke up and couldn't go back to sleep so I went for a walk. I wanted to clear my head."

"You don't leave the house this late at night! You were in bed all day because you've been"—and she uses those annoying air quotation marks here—"'sick' . . . and now you're out doing God knows what, acting like everything in the world is just fine?"

"I went for a walk. Around the block, okay? For twenty minutes. Can I go to bed, please? I'm tired."

"That is totally not the point! Anything could have happened to you this late at night. This is not something that you do!" She glares at you, and you don't answer her. You feel like you might cry.

She senses your tears coming and softens her tone. "Honey, are you okay? Is there something more going on? Do you need to talk about anything?"

She looks deep into your eyes like she's pleading with you to tell her everything that's going on, but you haven't got it in you to tell her what's wrong. So you tell her the only thing you can tell her.

"Mom. I'm okay."

"Get some rest. You know I'm just worried about you, right?"

"I know, Mom. I'm sorry. I love you."

Because you do love her. You do. It's just so hard. So hard when the monster is telling you so many things. He's telling you not to eat, he's telling you to hurt yourself, he's telling you to push away the ones you love, he's trying to ruin your life. And he's succeeding.

"I'm sorry I scared you."

"Go to sleep, honey. I love you too."

Saturday morning you ask your mom if you and Ben can go to Lake Pleasant for the day on Sunday to hike and swim. She hesitates for a moment but then agrees on the condition that you eat breakfast and wear plenty of sunscreen. You tell her you've already promised Ben that you'll eat breakfast too. You see your mom suppress a smile and you take that as a good sign.

Friday night when Ben asked you to eat breakfast before the hike, you said you would, and he asked what you might have.

"I eat breakfast. Breakfast isn't hard," you told him. "I eat waffles like it's my job." You smiled, and it felt wonderful to do that. To *smile*.

"Okay, eat waffles like it's your job on Sunday morning because you'll need a lot of energy for hiking. What do you want for lunch? I'm going to pack a lunch."

"A picnic?" you asked.

"Yeah, a picnic. Haven't you ever been on a picnic?" he asked.

"Not with a boy I like," you told him.

"I like you too," he said.

"You do?"

He touched his finger to your nose and kissed your lips softly. Then he said, "Very, very much."

38

Sunday turns out to be a beautiful day and when you arrive at Lake Pleasant you get out of the car and stretch your arms wide into the sunny, open skies. It's under one hundred degrees, which means it's actually cool, and Ben grabs his backpack and another one that he's packed for you. You're not a big fan of hiking but you've decided that if you're doing something with Ben, even if it's walking on fiery charcoals, you'll do it happily. Because you're with Ben.

You'd do anything with Ben.

"How many waffles did you eat this morning?" he asks.

"Promise you won't laugh?"

"Of course."

"Seven."

"Good Lord, woman!"

"You told me to eat a lot!"

"Is it that easy to get you to eat?" he asks.

"Maybe I don't need therapy," you say. "Maybe I just need you to tell me what to do."

"If only it were that easy," he agrees.

"Yeah."

"I wish I understood your eating disorder better," he says.

He leads you to the trailhead and you start on your hike, holding hands along the way. You feel like you want to tell him more, so that he understands.

"The stuff I did to my wrists and hands—which I've never done before, I want you to know that—and being mean to you . . . I'm not myself when that goes on, if that makes sense," you say.

Ben gives your hand an encouraging squeeze, so you continue.

"I feel restricted by this 'thing,' almost like there's a monster inside of me, telling me what to do, you know? And I'm sorry I've treated you so horribly when you've been nothing but amazing to me."

"No more *I'm sorry*s," he says, and he kisses the top of your head.

You tell Ben how you only think of food in negative ways, and how you wish you could change your behavior and rewire your brain.

"Is therapy not helping at all?" he asks.

"I'm not sure."

"Are you being open to it, I mean, really, really open to it?"

"I don't know."

"Maybe you have to be more open-minded to what they're trying to teach you," he says kindly. "But no more cutting. I don't want you to cut yourself anymore. The other night when

I saw that, well, it scared the crap out of me. When you left, I thought about it a long time." He says it in a tone that makes you feel a little anxious. You feel like he has more to say but you interrupt.

"I won't," you say. "I won't do it again." You hope you can keep that promise. You truly do.

"I'll try to help you any way I can. I may not say the right things all the time, or do the right things, but I care about you and want you to get better."

You smile. "I want that too." And you mean it. You actually feel the monster quiver. *Good*, you think. *Die*.

39

Ben takes you on a trail around the lake and he actually makes the hike fun. He holds your hand the whole time and leads you through the rocky terrain so you don't trip, which is your main reason for being apprehensive of hiking. That, and the fear of snakes. He assures you that if there's a snake he will fight it off for you. Actually, he promises if there's a snake he will help you get away from it so it won't bite you.

You trust him to keep his word.

There are no snakes.

Instead, you are surrounded by stunning lake views and desert foliage you rarely see near home: spindly saguaro, blooming cholla and organ pipe cactus, and colorful desert sage and marigold.

Ben pulls out his phone, clicks on his camera, and drapes his arm around you.

"Smile," he says.

You do, and he takes a few shots of the two of you, making sure to get the lake and mountain views in the background.

When he's done you both peer at the pictures, although they're hard to see in the sunlight. He chooses the best one, puts it on Instagram, and tags you.

"I'm hashtagging this one 'AwesomestGirlEver.'" He grabs your hand and pulls you forward to continue the hike. You're glad he's leading the way because if he could see the stupid grin on your face he'd tease you the rest of the day.

After you've hiked a while longer, Ben finds a clearing overlooking the lake where there are some large rocks and smooth ground, and he assures you it's a place snakes would not inhabit. He sets out a blanket for the picnic he's packed. He's got apple slices and carrots, peanut butter crackers, fresh bread, and small bottles of frozen water that have just begun to melt and are perfectly cold.

"You thought of everything," you exclaim.

"I even brought chocolate but that's for later."

"Did it melt?" you ask.

"I kept it near the chilled water bottles."

"You are brilliant," you say, because clearly, he is.

"What do you want to eat?" he asks.

You take a chunk of the bread and it's soft, safe, and delicious, and he has a sandwich that he's packed for himself. You eat the apple slices and carrots and then start in on some peanut butter crackers when you realize he's beaming at you.

"What?" you ask.

"You're really cute."

You laugh and nudge him with your shoe.

"You are," he says.

"What kind of sandwich is that?" you ask him.

"It's turkey with cheese."

"I wonder what would happen if I took a bite."

He lifts his eyebrows. "I thought you were a vegetarian?"

"Self-imposed," you say. You both laugh.

He hands you the sandwich and you look at it, and then take a bite. It's a small bite, mostly bread, but there's definitely some turkey and cheese in your mouth.

You chew.

You consider.

You try very hard not to think about what's in your mouth because if your brain and your mouth work too hard together then you know you'll gag.

You swallow quickly.

It tastes like . . . it tastes like nothing.

You tell him that and then you say, "It actually tastes a little like cardboard. Salty cardboard."

"Yeah, but look!" Ben says. "You took a bite! You chewed it, you ate it! And nothing horrible happened. That's awesome, babe!"

Now you're beaming.

You did it.

You pretty much know that this is what you'll need to do to conquer the monster.

You don't take another bite, but you feel like you've accomplished something. You feel great.

After lunch you clean up your stuff and head back down to the lake. You've got your my-mom-hates-this-suit suit on underneath your clothes. You strip off your shorts and watch Ben watch you as you take off your T-shirt.

"God, you're hot," he says.

He takes off his shirt and he's already got his board shorts on and you grin at him and say, "Nice abs." Then you run past him toward the lake because suddenly you're shy.

Ben follows you into the lukewarm water. You swim out neck-deep and tread water. Ben is tall enough to still stand and he grabs you around the waist immediately. You put your arms around his neck and there you both are, kissing, again.

You wrap your legs around Ben's waist and even though there are other people at the lake you don't care. Holding you, he walks farther out and off to the side, near a rock formation, and you keep kissing. The kissing is crazy, the water is glorious, there is a shock of blue sky and white clouds and the two of you are locked together, your lips exploring, your legs wrapped tight around him. Your heart is racing and you think, *ohmygod, ohmygod, ohmygod . . .*

You're so in love with this boy.

40

You text Jae on Sunday night.

How's your trip? You back yet?

No, tomorrow late. What's up?

Ben and I are back together!

Really! That's great! Can't wait to hear all about it!

OK. See you at school on Tuesday! ♥

Monday is Labor Day and Ben has stuff to do with his family so you spend the day catching up on homework. The good thing about Monday being Labor Day is that Healthy Foundations is closed so you don't have to go to therapy. You think that things are looking up for you until you get to school on Tuesday and get called to the office when you're in Math. Your teacher excuses you and the whispers in class erupt.

You can't imagine why you're being called to the office, other than maybe your mom forgot to call in your absence from Friday?

When you arrive at Reception, the secretary escorts you to the principal's office.

The small room is filled.

Your parents are there.

Your English teacher, Mr. Owens, is there.

There is another woman in the room you don't recognize.

You start to panic. Your breathing quickens and your heart smashes against your rib cage.

You've never felt fear like this.

The first thing you think is that Todd is dead.

"Please, have a seat," your principal, Mr. Jordan, says not unkindly, but it still doesn't calm your fears.

You sit in the chair between your parents, and your mom reaches for your arm.

And then you know.

You pull your arm away quickly but she grabs it again and looks at your wrist. Her face goes pale.

"Mom, it's not what you think!"

Mr. Jordan says, "We received an e-mail on anonymoustips.com that you might be having some trouble. The person who e-mailed indicated that you might be harming yourself."

You think back to English class last week. Who saw you? Alex watches you all the time, but the girl who sits next to you could have sent in the tip too. It could have been anyone in class. You're livid.

Your dad is looking straight ahead, grasping his hands

together tightly. His jaw is clenched and a vein in his neck is pulsing. You're not sure if he's upset or about ready to lose it.

"Daddy." It comes out sounding like a whimpering plea. "It's not what you think. Please, Daddy. I didn't . . . I promise you."

"Pea, honey, they're all here to help you." He cannot look you in the eyes.

Mr. Owens speaks up. "I read your six-word memoir last night. I'm just sorry I wasn't able to get to it until last evening because I was gone for the long holiday weekend. It caused great concern. *The monster inside wants me dead*?"

Mr. Jordan cuts in. "With that, and the anonymous tip that came in over the weekend, which we didn't see until staff checked the site this morning, we had to address this immediately."

Mr. Jordan nods in the direction of the nicely dressed woman. "Ms. Reynolds is from the Arizona Suicidal Crisis Management Team."

"Oh my God! I didn't try to kill myself!" You're reeling. You feel light-headed and your blood pulses through every vein in your body. Your adrenaline is at an all-time high.

Ms. Reynolds speaks then. "I'd like to take you to my office to talk, and then I'll evaluate what will happen next. You might need to go for some psychiatric care."

"What? Where?" You don't know what to think.

"We're here to help," Ms. Reynolds continues. "We only want the best for you."

"Where am I going? What . . . I didn't do anything wrong. I just have an eating disorder. That's all! Tell them, Mom! And I'm getting better! I am! I ate part of a turkey sandwich this weekend! Mom, I did!"

"Oh honey." Your mom begins to sob.

You cry hard, hot tears. The monster is looming large now, filling you with fear and anxiety.

He's going to end you.

"I don't want to go anywhere. I'm doing therapy with Shayna! I promise I wasn't trying to kill myself. I don't want to die. I just . . . I need help learning to eat, that's all!"

"Do you need to get anything out of your locker?" Mr. Jordan asks.

You think for a minute. This might be your only chance to talk to Ben.

"I have to get my backpack."

Mr. Jordan and Ms. Reynolds exchange glances. The principal nods his approval, and then says, "Your mom should go with you."

Your mom wipes away tears and you both stand up to go to your locker.

"Come back immediately," Mr. Jordan says.

"Yes, of course," your mom says.

You leave the office and you're still sniffling back tears. Your mom is silent.

"I can't believe you're doing this to me. You know I didn't try to kill myself," you tell her.

"I'm not doing anything *to* you. The school called this morning saying there was an anonymous tip that you've been cutting yourself. And that memoir? You say there's this monster and you need to die?"

"No, Mom. No! It's not like that!"

"Sweetheart, there is no alternative. Do you understand the severity of the situation? You need something more than Healthy Foundations. You're harming yourself, you're not eating, you're behaving erratically . . . Your father and I don't know what else to do."

"Mom, I don't want to die, it's just . . . it's just . . . I don't know . . ."

"We'll figure it out."

"Do you really think I'll have to be admitted somewhere?" The thought of it makes your head spin.

"I'm not sure, but something has to be done. Maybe they want to evaluate you overnight, that's all?"

"Okay." You feel a bit better now, thinking you might only be away for one night. When you get to your locker, you say, "I have to text Ben."

"I don't think that's a good idea, sweetie," your mom says.

"Why not? I need to tell him what's happening."

Your mom says, "All this cutting, this hurting yourself, it started when you met Ben. We're concerned that maybe a relationship is too much for you to deal with right now. Ms. Reynolds said I have to take your phone."

41

"You don't want to kill yourself?" Ms. Reynolds takes notes on a legal pad. The two of you are alone in her office while your parents wait in the lobby.

"Not yet," you say.

She glances at you from above her reading glasses. You realize that's not the right thing to say to someone on your crisis-management team, which she has told you she is a part of–the team. She is a member of your *crisis-management team*. If she's on your *team*, then why the fuck is she trying to get you committed? you wonder.

"I haven't tried to commit suicide," you say. "Ever."

"What thoughts do you have?" she asks.

"About what?" you ask.

"About life," Ms. Reynolds says.

"I hate it most days."

"Why?"

"Because it sucks."

"What sucks about life?" she asks.

"Everything," you answer.

"Some examples?"

"Let's see, my mom drinks more than she should. When my dad's not at his sports job, he's at home watching sports or talking to my brother about sports. My brother is an inactive participant in our family. But my dad thinks he walks on water. I can't eat. I have this thing where I hate food. I can't comprehend what it's like to enjoy eating. Now you all think I tried to commit suicide. The only thing I have going for me is a great boyfriend and apparently my parents think he's a bad influence on me."

You cross your arms defiantly and instantly feel like a snotty teenager.

"Anything else?"

"None of this is because of Ben. It's all because of the monster."

"Your English assignment monster?" Ms. Reynolds puts her pen down and gives you her full attention.

You sigh. You're so tired of everything. You're upset and exhausted, so you say exactly what you shouldn't.

"Yes, and I don't want to die. But the monster wants me dead."

"What do you mean?"

"I have a monster living inside me that constantly tells me what to do, what to think, how to behave, who to love, how to act, how to react, what and when I should eat. It's this monster that makes me do this bad stuff to myself. He makes me depressed, he makes me anxious. He controls my moods and my emotions, my anger and my sadness. I've had it, or him, my whole life."

"Go on."

"If you ask me if I want to kill myself, the answer is no. If you ask me if I want to live with this monster for the rest of my life, the answer is no. So there's that. If that's the choice I have, to have this monster in me for the rest of my life, then I don't want to live any longer."

As soon as you say the words, you realize you have sealed your fate.

Next, it's your turn to wait in the lobby. The walls are lilac and while you're sure it's supposed to be a soothing color, all you can think about is Easter eggs. There are motivational phrases painted in fancy script that say, *Just Breathe* and *Simplify* and *Keep Calm and Carry On*. You want to throw up. Actually, you want your safety pin so you can scratch a new pathway onto the back of your hand, somewhere fresh, so you can pull out some of the anxiety you're feeling. You want to scratch, scratch, scratch away everything that has happened this morning.

Your parents and Ms. Reynolds come out after about twenty minutes and you know it's not good. Your mom's eyes are rimmed red and she's got tissues balled up in her fist. Your dad looks like his favorite football team lost the Super Bowl. Your mom sits down next to you, your dad next to her, and Ms. Reynolds kneels in front of you.

You're ready but you're not.

"So sweetie," Ms. Reynolds begins, and you want to spit in her face when she calls you sweetie. "I discussed options with your parents and we all agree for now that you should probably go to St. Joe's for a short stay."

You begin to shake. The whole inside of your body goes hot and then numb. The monster roars ecstatically.

You try to gain some composure. "What about my therapy? I'm trying so hard with it. Shayna's helping me."

"When you get out, you'll be able to continue with your other therapy. Inpatient is just more structure, a quicker fix, with faster results to get you the help you require."

"How long?" You look at your parents. "Mom, Dad? How long?"

They look at each other, not wanting to answer, and Ms. Reynolds speaks. "Inpatient is usually only four to seven days in a case like yours. They'll teach you some very useful coping skills, how to handle your anxiety and depression, and they'll get you on the right medication. You'll be able to talk with other kids who have some of the same issues as you do." She pauses. "Remember, we're here to help you."

You're shaking your head back and forth, back and forth. You don't know if you'll be able to get through this.

42

Ms. Reynolds says goodbye and assures you that she'll see you at St. Joe's at the end of the week for an assessment meeting. Your parents take you to the hospital. You don't even get to go home. That's one of the rules with inpatient. You do not pass Go. You go straight to the psych ward. Because that's really what it is. A place for crazies.

You don't talk to your parents on the way to the "hospital" as they call it, although you know it's the Crazy House. You're scared to death, because you've seen movies about crazy people and you know it's all just about taking your meds in small paper cups and wearing hospital gowns and maybe even getting strapped to your bed at night. And freaky people shouting out the answers to *Jeopardy!* every evening, and crappy food they might shove down your throat to force you to eat.

You're pretty much terrified of what's about to happen.

For over an hour you sit in a room with your parents while a woman processes your admittance. She asks your parents a bunch of questions about your health and mental status while completely ignoring you. Then she hands a bunch of forms to your parents to fill out and leaves. You feel like you're about to have a panic attack. It doesn't help that the room is slightly larger than a public restroom.

The woman comes back in to get the forms and offers you water. You don't want to accept anything but you're parched so you take the water and drink it.

"We're almost done here," the woman says, and then she leaves again.

Your parents try small talk while you wait, saying things like, "This is going to be just fine," and, "You'll be so much better after this," and, "It's going to go by so quick, you'll see," but you ignore them. After a while your mom starts to quietly cry.

You're glad. You want her to feel pain. You doubt she or your dad have ever felt the pain you're feeling right now and you want to inflict some of it on them.

You think about Ben.

You think about how you were together at the lake on Sunday, how he held you in the warm water and kissed you, and pushed your wet hair away from your face and wiped the water from your eyes, how you wrapped your body around his and never wanted to let go, how you felt the safest and happiest you've ever felt.

He has no idea what's going on, or where you are, or where you're going to be for the next four to seven days. And you have no way to let him know.

The woman comes back and says someone will be there in

a moment to get you. She says good luck and leaves. While you thought your adrenaline couldn't spike any higher, it does. A staff member comes to get you and your parents. He takes you into the area that's the living space for the crazy people.

You can't get over the fact that this is where you'll be staying for however long they keep you here.

The staffer has a name tag that says DAMIAN and you can't help but think of some devil-worship guy because of his name. He's wearing jeans and a blue T-shirt that says, *Nobody Is Perfect, I Am Nobody.* He's got small gold studs in his ears and a sleeve of colorful tattoos with mostly skulls and some inspirational words on his forearm. When he speaks, he's not scary-sounding like you expected, so it calms you down, which is good, considering he's your first introduction to the Crazy House.

"Hey, I'm Damian, and I'll be here on shift for the rest of the day and part of the evening. I'll help you with anything you need, okay?"

You nod, then look at your feet. Because you're pretty scared, and nervous too, but you don't want to cry. You'll cry later. Later, you'll cry a ton.

"I do need your shoelaces, all of your jewelry, and are you wearing a belt?"

You consider this for a moment, and look at him.

"For safety reasons," Damian says.

Oh for God's sake.

"So I don't kill myself while I'm in here?"

"Pea!" your dad reprimands.

Damian grins. "You got it, girl."

This makes you like Damian a bit now, because he calls you girl, and because of his grin. He has really straight white teeth. You can tell he has good oral hygiene.

You remove the shoelaces from your Chucks, then you take out your earrings, remembering how Ben kissed you behind your earlobes on Sunday. You take off your necklace. It's a plain silver one you put on that morning.

"Do you have a phone?" he asks.

"They already took it away."

"Okay. Visiting hours are from six to seven every evening. Parents or guardians only."

"Great, that'll make Todd happy," you say.

"Who's Todd?"

"My brother. He hates me. But I can't see my boyfriend?"

"I'm sorry, no. But you can call him from seven to eight when the phone is free," Damian says.

You look to your mom and dad like you need approval. When they don't say anything, you say, "Mom, Dad, Ben has *nothing* to do with this. He's been helping me! He helped me eat turkey the other day! He was upset too. And he told me I need to go back on my meds. He's just as upset about this as you guys are!"

"You stopped taking your meds?" your mother asks, and then she looks down because her eyes fill with tears again.

You've had enough. You're sick of your parents, tired of the day's events, and you want to go to sleep. You feel like you could sleep forever.

"I'm exhausted." You look at Damian.

"Well, we have to take you to the nurse for a physical evaluation and then I'll show you to your room. You can meet your roommate and maybe rest a bit."

Shit. A roommate.

"It's time to say goodbye to your parents. They can come back tonight at six," Damian says.

Because you are all sorts of tired and angry and mixed-up and confused, you look at your mom and dad and say, "Can you come back tomorrow night instead? And bring me my pillow and some clean clothes." To Damian: "Am I allowed to have my pillow and my own clothes?"

"Yes."

"Then come back tomorrow night, please. I'm tired."

Your parents hug you and then you watch as they head toward the long hallway to freedom. Your mom is crying hysterically and your dad puts his arm around her shoulders and she falls in to him. You can't believe your mom is acting this way.

Why is she so upset? How is this making her so sad?

She's the one who's leaving you.

Your parents leave you at the Crazy House with Damian.

43

When you get to the nurse, whose name is Janet, the first thing she does is pull your wrists toward her so she can examine them.

"It's nothing, see? I just scratched on them a little. It calmed me down when I did that," you explain.

Janet glances up. "You can talk in therapy about why you did what you did, okay, hon?"

"Okay," you answer obediently. You're planning on being as agreeable and pleasant as you're able so you can get out of here as soon as possible.

She then checks your blood pressure, heart, ears, nose, throat, and reflexes, and then the questions begin.

"Are you on any medication?"

You tell her you were on Zoloft and it was working but you're no longer taking it.

"How much were you on and when did you stop taking it?"

"I think I was taking one hundred milligrams and I stopped taking it by accident. I met my boyfriend and started feeling happy. I forgot to take it and then still felt happy and figured I didn't need it."

She nods. "I'll check with your primary doctor to make sure you were at one hundred milligrams." Then she jots some info down. "Stopping your medication might explain some of your erratic behavior."

You decide you don't like this lady at all.

"I'm going to need to draw blood," she announces.

"How come?"

"To make sure you're getting the nutrients you need, to check your iron and potassium, make sure you're not under the influence of any drugs and that you aren't pregnant. I'll also have to scan your body for other self-inflicted injuries and check for lice."

"You're kidding, right?"

"Not kidding," Janet says. "Have you ever done drugs?"

"I don't do drugs!"

She squints at you and then asks, "Are you lying to me?"

"No! I don't even drink alcohol! Why didn't you ask me this stuff when my parents were here?"

"Children tend to lie when their parents are around. They seem to be more honest when their parents leave. Are you sexually active?" she asks.

"What do you mean?"

Janet gives you a look like you're in second grade, like duh, do you need to have the "talk," and then you say, "I've never had sex."

"Hmm." You can tell she thinks you're lying. Then she says,

"Sexual relations during your stay will result in immediate solitary confinement, so don't even consider it."

You can't even. This woman is the devil.

"You need to be aware of the rules."

She hands you a paper robe, tells you to change into it, and then heads to the door.

"I'll give you a couple minutes to change."

"Why do I have to change my clothes?"

"I told you. I have to check to make sure you haven't injured any other parts of your body. I can't do that with your clothes on. I'll be back in a minute. Tie goes in the front."

Janet leaves and you put on the robe, but then you curl up in the corner on the floor with your legs pulled up to your chest, and you start crying. You didn't sign up for this. This woman shouldn't be working at the Crazy House; she should be admitted. She's nuts.

The monster is roaring, and you feel a hotness inside you've never felt before. You're imagining having to stand naked in front of this horrible woman as she checks you all over for marks that don't exist. You feel like you're about to be violated.

Then the doorknob turns and Janet's back and another woman is with her.

You can't.

You won't.

You don't want to be here. This isn't what you deserve. You haven't done anything wrong.

"You have to get up; I have to take a quick look," Janet says.

Her voice sounds far away, the monster roars, and you're crying hot, heavy tears, shaking your head back and forth, back and forth. "No, no, no ... I can't, please, I don't want to do this!"

You heave and cry and rock, because you don't want this to be you. You don't want to be here, in this place, in this mess, having these strangers look at your naked body.

"Look, if you get up, we can do this really quick and painless."

The other lady comes over and kneels down by you.

"Sweetie, it'll be really quick, and you don't have to take the robe all the way off," she says.

"I don't?" you ask.

"No, come on, get up. I'll help you."

She seems a lot nicer than Janet, whom you hate with a burning passion, and you want this to be over with, so you take the nice lady's hand and you stand up and focus on her, whom you are now going to think of as Nice Lady during this whole process to make it go by faster.

Janet quickly scans your legs while Nice Lady talks to you, although you don't even know what she's talking about—she's really good at keeping your mind focused on something—and then you feel Janet's hands run along the length of your arms and you quiver with a hotness you hadn't expected. You hear Janet say, "No bruises or lacerations on forearms."

Then Nice Lady says to you, "I'm just going to untie the front and we're going to check your tummy and then your back and we'll be all done, okay?"

You nod, and then you hear Janet say, "Nothing here" and "Back is clear too," and, just like that, it's over. And Nice Lady is smiling at you and tying the paper robe back up.

"That wasn't too bad, was it?" Nice Lady asks.

You shake your head no.

Then Nice Lady smiles at you and leaves the room.

Janet then checks your scalp and says, "No lice eggs." Like you were expecting to be told otherwise. She takes five vials of blood from a vein in your right arm and wraps a blue bandage around your arm tightly.

"And we're all done!" Janet says cheerfully.

You say nothing.

"You can get dressed now," she says, and leaves the room.

After Janet is gone, you get dressed quickly and go out into the hallway where Damian is waiting for you with one of his bright, straight-teeth smiles.

On your way to your room, you check out his tattoos–there are some skulls. Hearts. A rose. The word *hope*. You focus on the word *hope*, although you feel numb.

All you want to do is crawl into a bed.

In your room, the walls are not cinder block, which you were expecting, but they are white. Damian explains that the door must remain open at all times, which relieves you because then your roommate can't kill you in the dead of night. It's a cold, basic room with a rectangular window you can't even get a view from—it's too high up. The two beds, on opposite walls, are covered with navy spreads and each has one white pillow at the head. There is a dresser with three drawers between the beds and another matching dresser along the wall where the door opens. A bathroom is near the door. The floor is linoleum and you wonder if that's for easy cleanup from the suicides and murders.

You stare at Damian because he's got to know this isn't where you belong. He's looking at you with kind eyes, gentle eyes, as if he knows what's going on with you, as if he truly understands that you're really scared.

He says, "Play your cards right and you'll be out of here in the minimum amount of time."

"This is crazy, right?" you whisper.

"I know it's tough. Do what they say, and everything will be fine."

You want to believe him so badly.

"Where's my roommate?"

"She's out in the common room, watching TV."

"Is she scary?" You're so afraid.

"Nah. Just don't stare into her eyes for too long."

You can't tell if he's joking, but then he grins really wide and you see his straight white teeth again. You exhale.

"What do I do now?"

"Well, dinner's at five, visitors come at six, and then you can make personal calls at seven," Damian says. "But you only get six minutes, and it's first come, first serve. It gets pretty busy during phone hour."

"Thanks for telling me."

"You'll be okay," Damian says.

"I need to lie down. Can I take a nap?"

"Sure, I'll see you later." And with a quick wave, Damian leaves your room.

You crawl into what you assume is your bed since the bed on the right has slippers on the floor nearby and a robe at the end of it. You put the pillow over your head and dream of Ben.

44

"It's dinnertime."

The girl is standing over you, staring at you as you move from sleeping to waking. You had been dreaming that you and Ben were hiking up a hill and were about to fly over a shimmering, glistening lake. Now some strange girl wearing a Hello Kitty T-shirt is demanding you get up for dinner.

"Huh?" You're confused, lost in the memory of your dream of Ben, not fully aware of where you are.

"Dinner. Five o'clock. I'm Savara."

"Hi," you say.

"What's your name?"

"I'm Pea."

"Pea? Is that short for something?"

"Just Pea." You decide that no one here is going to learn your real name. Ever.

She turns away from your bed and you sit up. She's got skinny jeans on to go with her Hello Kitty T-shirt and she's wearing dirty socks. She's scrawny, pale white, and delicate as a piece of loose-leaf paper. You can see right through to the veiny makeup of her insides. You're guessing drug addict, if you had to choose Reason for Admittance. Then you wonder if she's wondering about you.

And she is, because her next question is this:

"Why are you in here?"

You rub the sleep from your eyes and wonder the same thing. *Why am I in here?*

"I'm not entirely sure. I don't think I belong here." Then you realize how that sounds and you try to retract the words when Savara scowls at you.

"I . . . uh . . . I don't mean it like that. It's just, someone called in an anonymous tip at school about me and now everyone thinks I'm suicidal. That's why I'm here."

"Oh."

She's not buying it.

Then Savara says, "It'll all come out in therapy anyway. It always does. Get up. We have to go to dinner. If we're late, they mark it in our files."

You follow her out of the room to the dining area, which is near the lounge area. The shiny aluminum tables are long and seating is bench style. Everything is bolted to the floor. You guess it's so no one can hurl furniture at people. By the looks of it, there's room for about fifty people, tops. There are about twenty kids there—in one section there are younger kids who all look to be about six to twelve years old. Savara takes you through the food line and dinner is served to you on a Styrofoam plate by someone behind a glass window. Your meal consists of a piece of lasagna, some wilty salad, a roll with a pat of butter, and a brownie. There is a carton of milk too. You get to eat with a spork. No knife. Of course, because you could try to kill yourself with a plastic knife.

You feel sick to your stomach.

Savara sits next to a group of odd-looking teens and you sit next to her because what other option is there.

"New girl." Savara nods in your direction and you glance at each of them quickly, but don't really look at them yet. Then she says, "Her name's Pea."

A couple of the kids say hi, and one of the guys grunts his greeting, and then they all continue to talk as if you aren't there. They eat their food like it's no big deal, like it might even taste okay. You take this time to look at everyone.

There's a black girl with tragically straight hair and tons of split ends, faded red like she dyed it at home from a box, but did a terrible job. Next to her is a boy who looks to be the youngest—maybe thirteen—he's also black and he's rapping to some music in his head in between bites of his lasagna.

Across from Savara sits the most angry-looking guy you've ever laid eyes on. From the looks of him, he's exactly who you'd expect to be in the Crazy House. Dark clothes, dark hair, dark demeanor. You can tell he's had his lip and eyebrow pierced, and he's got about eight holes in each of his ears. His eyes are a fierce color of green, mesmerizing and eerie at the same time– you don't want to stop staring, although he looks like he could tear you apart with one scowl. You can also tell he's been hurt more than anyone deserves to be hurt. He stares back, challenging you, and you glance away.

At another table there is a group of kids who are loud and laughing and you can't believe that there is laughter in this place. That people can be happy in here. You're curious as to what makes them feel that way.

You pretend to busy yourself with your spork, like it's the most interesting thing you've ever seen. The monster is whispering something to you but you're not sure what he's saying. Maybe, *You're hungry, you're hungry, you're hungry.* Or, *You're trapped, you're trapped, you're trapped.*

Either one, he's right.

You take the roll and pick off a piece. You place the bit of bread in your mouth and chew.

Now everyone is staring at you.

"So," the black girl says, "what got you sent here?"

You swallow the bread and feel tears welling in the corners of your eyes.

She's not being mean. She's just asking a question.

"I guess I might have tried to kill myself." Although you know it's not true. You didn't *try* to kill yourself. But it's easier than attempting to explain everything to a bunch of strangers.

It's actually easier than the truth.

The others at the table nod. Like they know.

You take another piece of your roll. Your stomach growls so loud that everyone at the table hears it and they laugh.

"Damn, girl, you're hungry!" Savara says.

You look down at your plate. You will not eat the lasagna, and the salad looks pretty disgusting. You will finish your roll and eat the brownie though.

The black boy speaks. "I'm Malik. I tried to do it too. Three times. I thought the third time would be my ticket out. My grammy finally had enough and brought me here."

"Next time, Malik, tie that rope tighter." It's the green-eyed boy who says this. He's staring directly at you even though he was addressing Malik.

"Nah, man," Malik says. "Rope's too hard."

Green-eyed guy laughs. Then to you he says, "What about you?"

"Me, what?" you ask.

"How?" he says.

You pull your wrists quickly under the table and shake your head. "I don't want to talk about it."

He shrugs. "You just told me."

Savara says, "You're going to have to talk in group. They make us all talk. If you don't talk, you don't leave."

45

After dinner, parents arrive to see mostly the little kids. Savara doesn't get a visitor and neither does the black girl, whose name is Starling. Malik's grandmother comes to visit but green-eyed fierce boy doesn't get a visitor either. He goes to his room, and since doors have to stay open at all times, you can see him lying on his bed from the lounge area, where you sit with Starling and Savara. The lounge area isn't very "loungey" because the chairs are more like Lego blocks lined up in rows, bright yellow and red and blue. They're also bolted to the floor. There are a couple of throw pillows to try to give it a homey feel, but this place feels nothing like home.

There is an episode of *Full House* on TV and you wonder how none of those girls ended up in the Crazy House, living there with that nut job Uncle Joey with his cut-it-out shtick and the OCD dad who was always cleaning the house.

Savara and Starling tell you about the routine of the days: how you have breakfast, then there is therapy, then lunch, and some outdoor time, quiet time, and more therapy . . . It sounds pretty bleak to you. You see that the boy with the green eyes has shifted his position and has now moved to the end of his bed. He's on his stomach, his head resting on his hands, and he's staring at you.

You nudge Savara. "Why's he doing that?"

"Oh, Chad? He's just weird," she says. "He tries to intimidate all the new kids. Especially the girls who are cute."

"What's his deal?"

"His dad beat him up pretty bad. His mom was an alcoholic."

"Was?"

Starling and Savara exchange looks. "His dad killed his mom," Savara says.

Your eyes go large. You turn your head to Chad's room and look at him. He's staring at you still, but this time you hold his gaze. This time you don't see him as intimidating or fierce. This time you see Chad as a boy with his own monsters.

Damian comes by after all the parents leave. You're still watching TV with Savara. Starling has gone to her room.

"How are you doing?" he asks. "She teaching you everything you need to know?" He nods in Savara's direction.

"We're busting out at midnight." Savara smiles.

"Watch it," Damian says, laughing.

"I'm fine," you say.

"I came by to tell you that you can make a call now," he says.

A smile spreads across your face. "Really?"

"Sure. There's a line, but you can wait your turn."

You're dying to talk to Ben. He has no idea what's going on. This day has gone on forever. And you want this nightmare to be over with. At least, you think, you're almost through with Day One in the Crazy House.

You also want to call Shayna because she needs to know what's going on and you're not sure that your mom would have called her. You're positive you don't need to be here—you're not suicidal, so the people here are not going to help you. Shayna's going to help you. You need her. You need the therapy at Healthy Foundations. You don't need the Crazy House.

But first . . . first you need to talk to Ben.

You get up from the Lego chair and wave bye to Savara. As soon as you stand up to leave, Chad readjusts his position on his bed so he's no longer looking out into the lounge area.

Damian takes you to the phones and there is a line of kids waiting for the two available phones. You're praying these kids hurry up because it's already seven-thirty. A little girl who is about seven is on the phone begging to go home. "I don't like it here, Mommy," she cries. She wipes her nose with the back of her hand. Finally, a nurse takes the phone from her and tells her mom that yes, her child is fine, and she can come tomorrow at visiting hours.

Three more children make calls and then a teenager who you haven't seen before gets on a call. Two kids get tired of waiting and leave the line. Then it's your turn. You pick up the phone and you're sweating and shaking and praying. You dial Ben's number, and then you hear his beautiful voice. Like magic.

But it's his voice mail.

"Hey, it's Ben, leave a message and if you're lucky, I'll call you back."

Your voice cracks as you try to form words but all that comes out is: "Ben."

You can't think clearly and you want to get the words right, but you're not sure what to say, what to tell him. So you tell him only what you're sure of. "Ben, it's me. My parents had me admitted to St. Joe's. I can only call you between seven and eight. Can you call my mom? She'll tell you more. They sent me away. And I'm so scared."

You rattle off your house phone number and tell him you miss him so much. Then you hang up the phone and start to cry.

46

The next morning you wake and for a split second you don't remember where you are or what happened. Then the realization hits when you see Savara sleeping in her bed. You have no idea what time it is, but you hear some activity in the lounge area so you slip out of bed. Since you don't have any clothes other than the ones you arrived in, Damian gave you a hospital gown to sleep in, which leaves your back bare. You grab the blanket from your bed and wrap yourself in it for coverage and warmth and go out to the Lego chairs.

Chad is reading a book.

"Hi," you say.

He nods in your direction but continues to read.

You sit on a yellow Lego chair. He's sitting on a blue one.

"What do we do today?" you ask, even though the girls clued you in last night.

Without taking his eyes away from his book, he says, "Food, talk, food, minimal sunshine, lots more talk. If you have a book"– he lifts up his book–"you get to read."

"How long have you been here?" you ask.

"About eight days."

"Oh."

He continues to read and you watch him. You can smell food from the kitchen, but it doesn't mean anything to you.

Since you can't think of anything to talk about, you ask, "When are you getting out?"

"Dunno."

"I can tell you're not mean."

He nods. Then he says, "I'm not really here to make friends."

"Shit. I don't even want to be here," you say.

"Agreed."

"What are you reading?"

"*Catcher.*"

"*In the Rye?*"

"Is there any other *Catcher?*"

"I hated that book."

"Me too."

"Why are you reading it then?"

"Today's literary options were *Harry Potter* or *Catcher,* and I hate Harry more than Holden."

"Me too."

He lowers the book and slips his eyes above the top and you see the start of a grin form on his lips. You might have just won him over.

"So last night you said you 'might' have tried to kill yourself. What's that mean anyway?" Chad asks.

"I think it was more I was trying to cope, you know? And now I guess my parents are worried that I might be suicidal."

"Are you?" he asks.

"Am I what?"

"Suicidal?"

"I don't think so. I didn't actually try to kill myself. I've just got a mess of other problems. And being stuck here is one of the biggest of them all."

Chad nods, and then turns back to his book. He's done talking to you.

A couple other kids come out of their rooms and someone turns on the TV so your conversation is over. Savara comes out and sits next to you. "Hey, you wanna borrow a clean T-shirt until you get some fresh clothes?"

"Sure, that would be cool."

You had no idea that screwed-up kids could be so nice, you think, as you follow Savara back into your room. She grabs a T-shirt and hands it to you. It's an Elmo *Sesame Street* shirt.

"Remember," Savara says, "Elmo loves you."

"Thanks," you say, laughing. This is one monster you actually like.

You take off the hospital gown and put on the Elmo shirt and your shorts from yesterday.

"So you and Chad have a deep conversation this morning?" she asks.

"Kind of," you say. "Turns out we both hate *Harry Potter.*"

Malik isn't at breakfast. You don't think it's anything strange, because you don't know how things work here. But then Savara says, "If you're late for breakfast, they mark it in your file, and if you get three late checks, it's bad news. *Bad* news."

There is some whispering among staff and then someone's radio buzzes, alerting them to meet in the main lobby. An announcement over the loudspeaker mandates that all patients remain in the dining area. You were almost excited about eating pancakes for breakfast but now there's a sinking feeling in the pit of your stomach when all the adults except for one guard head to the lobby.

You know something bad has happened.

The silence is eerie.

"We should eat," Starling finally says. You pick up your spork to eat the pancakes. It's a food you like, one you can actually eat, so you do. Because you have no idea what lunch might be, and judging from last night's dinner, the meals are not going to be things you can tolerate. You eat all three of the pancakes.

The only thing you can hear is the scraping of sporks along Styrofoam.

None of the staff has come back and it's been fifteen minutes since the announcement was made.

"What do you think happened?" you ask. "Where do you think Malik is?"

Starling, Savara, and Chad shrug. There are two other teens sitting with you and you don't know them, but one of them offers, "Maybe he did it, killed himself."

You swallow hard at the thought.

Finally, the kitchen staff comes in and they go back to their positions, and some of them start cleaning up. Someone else comes in and says, "Therapy at ten, guys. Teens in Room 100. Under twelves, you go to the rec room."

No one says anything else and you pick up your tray and throw out your trash.

At your first official therapy session in the Crazy House, your suspicions are confirmed.

"I have some very sad news," your brand-new therapist, Dr. Lawrey, announces. "Malik committed suicide last night."

Starling begins to cry, and Savara puts her arms around her.

Chad clenches his jaw and makes his hands into tight fists. "How?" he asks.

"This is a private matter that we can't discuss," Dr. Lawrey says.

You can't believe that this has happened. That you're here

because people are worried that you're a suicide risk and you're in a place where kids can do the job right under the noses of the people who are supposed to be protecting them.

You want the hell out of here *now*.

This may be the first time in your entire life that you are taking control over everything. Over the monster. You're not going to take shit from anyone any longer.

You stand up. "I need to call my parents. And my therapist. *Now.*"

47

You ask one of the nurses if you may use the phone.

"I'm sorry, you can only make calls at seven."

"But I need to talk to my mom."

"She'll be here at visiting hours tonight at six, right? You can talk to her then."

"Is Damian here?" you ask. You're positive he'll help you make a call to your mom. He'll help you get in touch with Shayna.

"He's working the evening shift."

Something in you rages. But this time, it's not the monster, and you feel this time it's something stronger. And you've never felt anything more powerful than the monster inside you. You start to scream at the top of your lungs, shouting and yelling, "Why won't anyone listen to me! I need to talk to my mother! I need to get out of here! I have to get out of here!"

Two male guards rush over and grab you and attempt to calm

you down, but you are so worked up and upset that nothing they do works. They threaten to put you in a room by yourself for the rest of the day, they threaten to give you a sedative, they keep throwing threats of all sorts your way until finally a well-dressed woman presents herself.

"Come with me," she demands. "Now."

You stop screaming and thrashing because she seems to have the authority that no one else possesses and you're hopeful that this woman can get you the hell out of here.

She takes you to an office filled with impressive mahogany furniture and all sorts of books about the injured child, the depressed child, the hurt child, the damaged child, the sad child, the unfortunate child. You sit and stare at all the titles of how pathetic you're supposed to be. Finally, she speaks.

"I'm Dr. Winthrop. Head of the hospital." She clasps her hands together. "We do not tolerate outbursts such as that. What happened?"

"I need my mom," you whimper.

"She'll be here at six," Dr. Winthrop says.

"No, you don't understand. I got placed here wrongly. I don't belong here."

She looks at you like she's heard this all too many times before, and she probably has, but you're certain they made a mistake with you. You have an eating disorder. You are not suicidal. You explain this to her.

Dr. Winthrop opens a file on her desk. "I understand you're

upset. And what has happened with Malik is devastating. I'm sorry this has upset you so much. This is a tragic event."

You sniffle and nod, and she hands you a box of tissues.

"But the fact remains that you're here for your own safety."

You can't help but think of what just occurred and how he wasn't safe. "What about Malik?" you ask.

"That's different," Dr. Winthrop says.

"How so? If you think I'm suicidal, how are you going to keep me safe?" you ask.

"Well, you said so yourself, that we have it wrong, and you're not a suicide risk, right?" Dr. Winthrop lifts her eyebrows. Point for Dr. Winthrop, you think.

"But if I don't want to kill myself, why are you keeping me here?" You think you've got her now and she'll have to let you go home.

She flips through your file. "You told Ms. Reynolds that you don't want to kill yourself 'yet.' That's a red flag, a very big warning sign. Also, a direct quote from your conversation with her: 'If you ask me if I want to live with this monster for the rest of my life, the answer is no . . . If that's the choice I have, to have this monster in me for the rest of my life, then I don't want to live any longer.'"

You don't say anything and she takes out another piece of paper. You recognize your handwriting. It's from your English class. It's your six-word memoir. Dr. Winthrop reads it aloud:

"The monster inside wants me dead."

She shuts the file folder and looks for your reaction. You feel emotions but try so hard not to react. You look at your scratched fingernails, and at the cuts and scrapes along your wrists, fingers, and palms.

"Do you see that we only have the best intentions here? And that we are only trying to help, to keep you safe? We're trying to help. We really are. Whether or not you believe it, you need to be here, for your mental stability. That episode out there further proves it."

You shake your head back and forth, still looking down at your hands, and the tears fall. You don't make any noise at all. You feel defeated, like you have no chance of getting out, like you've just gotten a life sentence. You don't see how they can possibly help you, how they can get rid of the monster, how they can keep you safe when a kid just took his own life practically right in front of you.

"So we're good? You're ready to cooperate and make this work for you?"

You're not ready, and you're not good, but you don't know what else to do. You feel trapped, confused, stuck. You hope you can convince your mom and dad to get you out of this place tonight. Maybe you'll promise them you'll eat anything and everything they put in front of you, if only they'll take you out of this place. Because nothing in your entire life has felt as horrible as what you've experienced since you've been in the Crazy House.

And you don't think you can take any more of it.

You nod, but before Dr. Winthrop excuses you from her office, she has one more thing to say to you.

"And to be clear, one more episode like what you pulled out there, and there will be consequences."

48

Since you had your breakdown during morning therapy, you meet up with the others at lunch. You're shaken up and upset but you have to play by the rules if you want to get out of here. Savara pats the seat next to hers in the dining area after you've gotten your designated meal of a turkey sandwich, some sort of pasta salad, a Jell-O, and milk. The turkey sandwich makes you think of Ben and the picnic that you shared only a few days ago.

You miss him so much you sigh out loud.

The others mistake it for a reaction to what happened with Malik, which isn't altogether incorrect.

Starling can barely look at her food. "They made me come to lunch. I wanted to stay in my room, but they said I had to come eat," she says.

A kid you haven't met yet is sitting at the table. He's a bit overweight with black-rimmed glasses and an unfortunate complexion. He pushes his glasses up on the bridge of his nose and says, "I'm the one who found him. Malik was my roommate."

"Ken. Don't." Chad looks up from his plate, shaking his head. "Just don't."

Ken wipes the back of his hand across his nose and smirks at Chad.

"I woke up and he was in bed and I thought he was asleep. So I go, 'Hey, Malik, get up,' and when he didn't answer I went over there and his face was gray. I think he took a bunch of pills."

"Shut up!" Chad slams his fists on the table and stands up quickly and one of the kitchen staff comes over.

"Is everything okay here?"

Starling begins to cry and you start shaking. Savara whispers to Starling to try to get her to calm down.

"No," Chad says. "Ken's talking shit about Malik. And he's upsetting the girls."

"Ken." The staffer nods for him to get up. He moves Ken to an isolated table and watches over him while he finishes his lunch.

"Thank you," you say to Chad.

"That's just wrong," he says. Starling stops crying, takes a sip of her milk. "Malik was such a nice kid."

Chad nods.

You wish a place like this didn't exist.

You wonder if Malik is happy being dead.

After lunch it's recreation time but the mood is extremely solemn. Of course, since it's your second day at the Crazy House, you have no idea if recreation time is otherwise exciting, but you follow the others outside for fresh air and activity.

You're supposed to play badminton. Instead of a real game, you bat the little birdie thingy back and forth to one another while staff watch from the outskirts of the building. Sometimes someone gets angry and smashes the birdie at another kid, but for the most part, everyone is pretty melancholy.

"Why do you think he did it?" some boy you don't know asks. It's on everybody's mind.

Starling speaks first, after she sends the birdie across the net to you. "His mother sent him and his little sister to live with his grandmother—he said his mom couldn't afford to take care of them. And his grandmother was struggling. He felt like no one wanted him."

You think about this. Everyone in your life wants you in his or her life. Your mom, your dad, even your stupid-ass brother. As much as he is a stupid ass, you think he'd be devastated if you weren't around. Jae would die if you weren't here. And Ben, and the little bit you know about his family. They all want you around. You've got so much to be happy about.

Why aren't you happy? Why can't you be happy? Because of food? Because of the monster? Because of what happened with Alex last year? Because of rumors that aren't going to matter when you're done with high school?

How can you turn all of this around? How can you make the changes you need to make in your life and start being happy with yourself? With the gifts you've been given? With the things you have in your life?

These are some of the questions you're going to need to answer. If you want to get rid of the monster, and if you want to get out of the Crazy House and start living the life you deserve to live.

You've got to start digging deep. You know you don't belong in the psych ward. Starling, Savara, and Chad seem like good people, but you're pretty sure they've been damaged by circumstances beyond their control, and they need more help than you do. You want to get home to the people who are waiting for you, waiting to help you.

There's Ben too. And you need him.

49

Sleep comes easily that afternoon during break, and then there's a group session where a new therapist talks to you and the others about feelings and overcoming obstacles. She also talks about being mindful and in the moment and what it means to be present.

You wish you weren't present. You wish all of this were in your past.

After dinner, which you don't eat because it's chicken, you go into the lounge and sit at one of the benches at the long tables. Some of the younger kids have been here earlier and they've left coloring pages and crayons.

You pick up a crayon. It's the carnation-pink one. You smell it. It brings you right back to preschool and the feelings you had when you were little. When things were simple and easy. When your biggest worry was whether you wanted to color with the carnation-pink or the lavender crayon from your big box of Crayolas. When you hated to peel the paper off the crayon because the pointy crayon was turning into a nub and it was time to stick it in the back of the box and twist it in the sharpener.

Savara joins you, and she picks up a green crayon and reaches for a coloring page. She chooses a picture of Spider-Man.

You're coloring a Barbie page—she's in her convertible on a road to nowhere. It feels oddly like your life, except you're not perfect Barbie and you're not in a convertible, you just feel like you're going nowhere. You search for a yellow crayon and find canary and color the long strokes of Barbie's hair.

"You okay?" Savara finally asks.

You shrug.

"Today totally sucked," Savara says.

"Yeah."

"I'm leaving on Friday," she says. It's Wednesday night.

"Why're you here anyway?"

"I'm bipolar. I'm getting my meds adjusted. This is my third time here."

You both keep coloring. It's therapeutic. You feel your heart rate slow. This is the calmest you have felt since you got here.

"I'm sorry," you say.

"Well, hopefully they got my meds right this time," Savara says.

"Have you ever . . ." You don't want to finish the sentence but Savara knows what you're asking.

"I think about it. A lot. But no."

"Do you want to get better?" you ask.

"I do. I really do. It's just so fucking hard, you know?"

"I know."

You both continue to color and then it's six o'clock and the parents who have been waiting outside are allowed to come in. Savara's parents are here. Your parents are here. You get up and hug them, and your mom immediately bursts into tears so you do too.

Your dad wraps his arms around the both of you. "Don't cry, Pea, honey, it's okay."

You and your mom cling to each other for a while longer, and then she pulls away and wipes tears from your eyes.

The first thing you ask your parents is if Ben called the house. It's the most important thing you want to know.

"He did. Late last night," your dad says.

"You talked to him? What did you say? What did he say? Tell me!"

"I told him that you were here and we weren't sure when you'd be home but you're getting the help you need."

You don't exactly agree with this but you don't say anything about it.

"Did you call Shayna?" you ask next. "Does she know where I am?"

"Yes, she knows where you are. We've got her plugged into the situation." Your dad says this like he's reporting football scores. You want to smack him.

"Are you okay?" your mom asks. She brushes a piece of your hair away from your face.

"It's awful." You tell your parents how horrible your physical exam was.

"And I wanted to call you this morning but they wouldn't let me," you add.

It's as if neither of your parents knows how to respond. You keep talking.

"They don't even care that I have an eating disorder."

You have moved over to a quiet spot in the lounge, near the window, and you and your parents sit on three of the Lego chairs.

Your parents look at each other. You hope they are rethinking sending you here.

"I call these the Lego chairs," you say. "You can't move them. So no one can throw them if they get pissed."

Your mom looks shocked.

"Mom," you say, "don't worry about that. The only good thing is that the kids are nice." Then you tell them about Malik. They say they already knew. Dr. Winthrop came out and explained the situation to all the visitors before they were let in.

"It's so sad, Mom," you say. "He seemed like such a nice kid, but at dinner last night . . . God, it was *only* last night that he was alive . . . he said he'd tried to kill himself three times."

"Oh dear God," your father says. You wonder if your parents are beginning to see how crazy it is that they've sent you here, and that you don't need to be at the Crazy House. So you try to use it to your advantage.

"I shouldn't be here. No one cares that I have ARFID. They're not making sure I'm eating the right stuff or helping me get better. No one cares if I eat. You have to get me out of here."

Your parents exchange worried looks.

"Can't you call Shayna again, Mom? Can she do anything to get me out sooner? I want to go back to Healthy Foundations. I was trying hard, I really was. Shayna told me to expect ups and downs with therapy. Maybe the cutting was just part of the downs. I didn't mean to do it. Can you get Shayna to come here and talk to them?"

"Maybe," your mom says, but you're not entirely sure your mom believes you. Maybe your mom wants you to stay.

Your dad speaks then. "Pea, we are really scared that you're going to hurt yourself. We feel that you're safe here, despite what happened to Malik. We understand he was severely troubled. But you need to learn some skills and some ways to lower your anxiety. You haven't been yourself, and then that anonymous tip came in to school. We're concerned for your well-being."

"Dad!" Your voice has risen and the guard turns to see if there is a problem.

"What about the cutting though?" Your dad moves his body closer to yours and touches your hands and you instinctively pull away. "Clearly you're hurting yourself. You must have thoughts about hurting yourself?"

"I don't know," you admit.

"Why did you do it?" your mom asks.

"Mom. I don't know. It was stupid. I'm not going to do it anymore. I promise. It just . . . it just . . . it felt like it soothed me for the moment. I don't know. Maybe like how a glass of wine soothes you?"

You didn't want the words to sting her but you suspect they might. "I don't mean it in a mean way. And I know I shouldn't compare the two, but it calmed me down when I was feeling tense. And I know I need to find a better way to cope. I know that now. And I'm ready to figure that out. But this is not the place."

Your parents glance at each other again.

"Really, Mom, Dad. I don't need to be here."

You can tell your parents are considering your words.

"We all have a meeting with Ms. Reynolds and Dr. Winthrop on Friday. I'll see if it makes sense to have Shayna come," your mom says. "But until then, do whatever they say you need to do, okay?"

"Yes," your dad agrees. "Dr. Winthrop told us about your fit this morning. If you behave like that, they'll just have reason to tell us that you need to stay. Got it?"

"Dr. Winthrop is crazy," you say. "I just want to go home."

"You know we want you home too. More than anything," your mom says.

This makes you want to cry, but you hold it in. Your mom

hands you the duffel bag she brought with clean clothes, your pillow, and the toiletries you are allowed to have. You cannot wait to take a shower and shampoo your hair.

As visiting hour ends, your parents tell you they won't be by tomorrow night since they'll be here Friday for your assessment meeting. They hug you hard, tell you they love you, then they leave.

50

After your parents leave, you get in line for the phones but it seems as if everyone wants to make a call tonight. You wait and you wait, and there are still six kids in line at eight o'clock when phone time is over. You've missed your chance to call Ben.

"For those of you who didn't get to make a call tonight, you'll definitely get to call tomorrow night," the night nurse says. You're really bummed and feel like crying. You need to talk to Ben.

Savara and you settle in to watch *Full House*. It seems to be the thing to do, as several other kids have come to the lounge to watch TV too. At the first commercial you tell Savara you're going to the kitchen to get some water and you ask if she wants anything to drink.

"Nah, I'm good," she says.

"I'll be right back," you tell her.

The lights are on in the kitchen and Damian is at the sink washing his hands.

"Hey," you say. "Can I get a cup for water?"

"Sure. Styrofoam cups in that cabinet," he says, nodding to his left.

You pull out a cup and go to the machine for ice and water. "Nice shirt, by the way."

Damian looks down as if he doesn't remember what T-shirt he has on. It's one that says, *I'm with Handsome* with an arrow pointing up to his face.

"Oh yeah, well, it's true." He laughs. "Oh, I have something for you . . ." He wipes his hands on his jeans, reaches into his back pocket, and pulls out a folded envelope.

"Here you go. Almost forgot to give this to you."

He hands you the envelope.

"What is it?"

"Your boyfriend was here today."

"Ben?"

"If that's his name? I was taking the garbage out and this guy stopped me and showed me a picture of you on his phone—you two hiking? By the way, I so didn't peg you as the hiking type. Anyway, he asked if I knew you and if I would give you this letter. Offered me ten bucks."

You furrow your brow, imagining the scenario, Ben being here earlier in the day, maybe right after school, trying to find a way to get a letter to you.

"You know," Damian says, "he really shouldn't have been hanging around here. If Winthrop saw him, she'd probably find a reason to have him committed."

You laugh and take a sip of your water. "You're not kidding."

You slip the envelope into your pocket.

"For the record, I didn't take his money," Damian says.

"I knew you wouldn't. Thanks for getting it to me."

You head back to the lounge, the words from Ben tucked in your pocket.

You look for Savara to tell her about your letter but she's gone. The TV is still on, volume on High, but no one is watching anymore. Kids have moved to the table and they're coloring and playing checkers. You sit down on a chair, put your water on the table next to you, and pull the envelope out of your pocket to read Ben's letter.

Just as you start to open it, Ken, the nerdy fat kid who was Malik's roommate, comes up behind you and snatches the envelope out of your hand. He walks around and sits super-close to you on one of the chairs. He's creepy and his teeth are crooked and really yellow. And he's holding the only connection you have to Ben in his meaty hands.

"What's this?" He raises his eyebrows.

"Give that back," you snarl at him. He's bad news. He upset everyone at lunch this afternoon and now he's bullying you. "I need that back. Please." You try to look at him nicely even though you want to kill him.

Ken responds, "How bad do you want it?"

You can't believe he's bribing you. You stare at Ken, trying to figure out what to do while the laugh track of *Full House* plays.

He toys with the envelope. "What's this all about?"

He turns the envelope over in his hands, lifts it up to the light as if he's trying to read through it. "So what's it gonna be?" he asks. "Am I going to have to read it here, or do you want to make some sort of deal? I know where we can go do some negotiating."

You want to vomit. But before you can think of anything to say, Chad bolts out of his room and pulls the envelope from Ken's hands. You didn't realize that he was there, on his bed in the dark, watching this whole encounter unfold.

"Don't be a dick, Ken. You're such an asshole." Chad hands you the now-crumpled envelope. "Get out of here and find someone else to bully." Chad glares at Ken.

"I was just having some fun, I wasn't going to read it," Ken whines, then gets up from the Lego chair and skulks over to the benches where the younger kids are coloring.

"Oh my God, Chad, thank you so much," you say.

"No problem. That guy is such a douche."

"The worst."

"Yeah," Chad says. "Well, I'll let you get to your letter."

You stand up and before you leave, you give Chad a hug. "Thanks," you say. "That was awesome of you."

You go to your room, open the envelope, and take out the piece of paper. Your heart starts racing when you see Ben's words.

Babe,

(You love when he calls you babe.)

I miss you. I can't stand being away from you.

(Your stomach flutters like it did the first time you met him and he held your hand and you felt it all the way down to your toes.)

I need to hold you again. I need you in my arms.

(You too wish so badly that you could be with him, that you could hold each other.)

You'll be out of there soon. I promise. Then I can hold you and kiss you and love you.

Because I do. I love you. And I want you to know that. I wanted to tell you at the lake on Sunday and I should have. I love you.

Think of me when you go to sleep and when you wake up because I'll be thinking of you then.

I'll be waiting for you when you come home. I love you.

Ben

51

After breakfast on Thursday you thank Chad again for getting your letter back from Ken.

"No problem," Chad says. "I should have warned you about Ken sooner. Just stay as far away from him as you can."

"I'm hoping I won't have to deal with him much longer. I hope I get to go home tomorrow after my assessment meeting."

"It's tomorrow already?" he asks.

"Yep."

"Well, steer clear of him from now on. He's got his sights set on you for some reason."

"Thanks," you say.

Your day is busy—you have a therapy session on mindfulness and a morning break of a couple of eighties sitcoms, and then there's another lunch you don't eat—ham sandwich and potato salad. Then everyone heads outside for outdoor-activity time.

During the allotted twenty minutes of fresh air, there is a discussion of whether you should play badminton or basketball. No one wants to play either game. Instead you all lie on the concrete court, lapping up the warmth like a bunch of iguanas, like you may never get to see the sun again. It feels decadent to be outside, to feel the heat on your skin. It feels a bit like hope, like there might be a future.

"Is this what mindfulness feels like?" you ask.

"Are you being in the moment?" Savara jokes.

"I might be, actually."

"Are you not judging how the sun feels on your face? And just noticing it?" Chad chimes in.

You laugh. "Sure."

"Then I guess you're being mindful of what it's like to sit in the sun."

You think about this. Being mindful. The stuff they're shoving down your throat at therapy sessions. Being in the moment, not judging. Have you been judgmental? Of course. You immediately judge the girls on Instagram and Twitter, by what they say, by how they pose, by how they appear in their photos. You come to an instant conclusion about people by what they wear and how they look, and by what they say or how they act, and who they hang out with. You're trying to be mindful now but you're not too sure about this stuff. How is being "mindful" going to make you a less anxious or depressed person? You don't get it. Then you realize your mind is wandering.

"Oh shit," you say. "I stopped being mindful!"

Chad, Savara, and Starling laugh.

You close your eyes, letting the sun warm your face, and think of Ben. You miss him and can't believe what he wrote in his letter.

He loves you.

How can he love you when you've got the monster in the way, when you were so mean to him, when you can't promise you won't freak out on him again?

How can you be so deserving of him, of his love?

You're going to have to trust him. Trust his love.

You're going to have to be better to him.

You know your disorder—your monster—has prevented you from opening up to people whom you care about. You want to start being completely present and open with others.

Especially Ben.

You know you want Ben in your life. And you're getting stronger, you feel it. You've felt the monster settling down—even though you hate being in the hospital, something is changing.

You're just not sure exactly what. Maybe the desire not to be here is so strong, there's a shift inside of you to do something different, something big to change the way you've been living.

Maybe, just maybe, you are being mindful?

* * *

That night, after dinner, you and Savara are in your room. She's going through her things, which don't add up to much, just some toiletries and her clothes. You're sitting on your bed, watching her pack.

"What are you going to do when you go home?" you ask her.

"I'm going to go back to seeing my therapist. I think my parents want to send me to a different school. Which might be okay. There's been a lot of crap at my school. I think I need some new friends, better influences."

"Do you think you'll ever have to come back here?"

Savara looks at you and grins. "As much as I like you and don't want to leave you, I hope I never come back."

You laugh because it's so true. Despite only knowing Savara a couple of days, you've bonded quickly. The Crazy House will do that to people.

"You know I would have completely lost it in here without you," you tell her.

"You would have been fine," Savara says.

"Well, anyway, I'm glad you were here."

"Starling's gonna lose her shit when I leave tomorrow," Savara says.

"I'll keep an eye on her."

"You'll probably get out right after me," Savara notes.

You hope so. You hope you get to go home after your assessment tomorrow, which will be your fourth day here. You're ready to go home. You are ready to do whatever it takes to create a normal life for yourself, no matter what that might be.

Savara finishes packing and then you go out to make a call. You don't mind that your parents didn't come tonight because you'll see them tomorrow. You hope they've arranged for Shayna to be here.

But right now, all you can think about is calling Ben.

52

Ben answers the phone and just hearing his voice brings all your emotions front and center. Tears trickle down your cheeks and you sniffle back sounds of crying. You don't want to cry.

Immediately you apologize.

"It's okay," he says. Then, "I miss you, babe. Are you okay?"

"Yes." You wipe your nose and compose yourself. "Thanks for the letter. I love it," you whisper.

"I love you," he says. It's the first time you've heard him say it.

"I love you too." *I love you too.*

They are like magic words and you literally feel the monster shrivel inside of you. The power of the words, of having someone important love you and being able to love that someone back, it's not like it angers the monster into a rage, but it diminishes his power. It makes him seriously crumble a bit. You're taking away his power by loving and being loved. You're discovering this. That love can overpower the monster. You hold on to this information, knowing that it will be needed down the road when things are hard again.

"How are you?" Ben asks.

A calm has come over you and you tell him you feel okay, that you feel like you're getting well, and you want to get well, that you want to get out of here. That you don't hate it here, and most of the kids are actually very nice. You don't tell him about Malik because you don't want to cry anymore. You want to feel this happiness that's building. You want to keep it growing there.

"When will you be home? I miss you so much."

"Mom and Dad come tomorrow for a big meeting," you say. "I hope they'll let me leave with them."

"Me too," Ben says. "Then we could have the whole weekend together."

You think about this, to be able to spend the weekend with Ben. To hug him and kiss him and just see him. The thought makes you feel like you're going to get through this, knowing he wants you as much as you want him and that he's waiting for you.

One of the nurses taps her wrist, motioning that your time for the phone call is up.

"Ben, I've got to go. My time's up. Maybe by this time tomorrow I'll be home?"

"I would love that. I love you. I miss you. I love you." He says it twice.

Twice.

"I love you too."

53

Savara's parents come after breakfast on Friday to get her. You hug each other tightly and say goodbye. You think you probably won't ever talk to her again and you're pretty sad about that but you feel like people come in and out of your life for a reason and you know Savara helped you through a very difficult time.

It's weird having Savara gone and at lunchtime you feel her absence when it's just you, Chad, and Starling clustered at one corner of a table.

A new patient comes in and she sits by herself at the end of your table. You know without a doubt that if Savara were here, she would invite the girl over to eat with the group. You can tell she's lonely and scared, and she looks about your age, but you just haven't got it in you to invite her to sit with you. Later, you're going to feel guilty about ignoring the girl, but you're a bundle of nervous energy about the big meeting you have after lunch with Reynolds and Winthrop and you're in no mood to make small talk with a new person.

"Why're you so quiet?" Chad finally asks, between bites of ravioli.

Weird how after only four days he can tell how you're feeling.

"I'm nervous about my assessment meeting this afternoon," you admit.

"If they let you out, I'm gonna die in here!" Starling says dramatically.

"Shut up," Chad says. "That's not cool."

Starling lowers her head and pokes at her ravioli.

Chad turns his attention back to you. "They'll probably let you out. You haven't done anything wrong."

"I threw that huge fit on Wednesday," you remind him.

"But God, it was warranted, it was because of Malik," he says.

"Please!" Starling moans. "Don't bring up Malik!"

The new girl at the end of the table looks at the three of you.

One of the staffers walks over to your table to check in.

"Everything's fine, Rick," Chad says. "We're just sad about Malik." He nods in Starling's direction.

Rick nods and walks away.

Chad leans in to you and you search his green eyes, sensing he's going to say something very important. He does.

"Listen. If they ask you if you're having those thoughts anymore, tell them you're not. Tell them they're gone. Even if you still have them."

You hold his gaze and there's something deep and dark in

his eyes, something that makes you believe he knows what he's talking about.

"Even if you think about it for a split second *ever*, don't tell them." He comes closer to you and you feel his warm breath as he whispers in your ear. "If you do, they'll keep you here. I promise you that."

You pull back and get your focus, clear your head, and wonder if you're really having those kinds of thoughts anymore because you don't think you are. But you're not sure.

Chad picks up his spork, takes another bite of his ravioli, which has to be cold by now, and mouths one last word to you, but it's still very clear, although no one else hears it:

"Lie."

54

They're waiting for you in Dr. Winthrop's mahogany office—your parents, Dr. Winthrop, Ms. Reynolds, Horrible Janet the nurse, and Damian. You mouth to Damian, *What are you doing here?* and he whispers back, "Day shift, today and tomorrow." You're glad he's here even though everyone looks as if they're conducting an intervention on your life, sitting in big leather chairs. You feel like you should plant yourself right smack in the middle of the floor, front and center, and let them fire away at you.

Then you see Shayna and you feel a glimmer of hope spark in the center of your soul. If there's any chance of you getting out of here, it's Shayna. She, of all people, knows you're not crazy. She knows you're not suicidal. Shayna knows you only have an eating disorder. You're sure she'll get you out.

You take a seat between your mom and dad, the spot that you think is the safest in the room, and Dr. Winthrop begins with introductions. Then she dives right in and addresses you directly.

"We're all here because we care about your well-being, and we think you're in danger of harming yourself. High risk. That's why you're here," she says.

You stare at her.

"Have you realized that's the reason you've been brought inpatient?"

"I'm not going to kill myself. I didn't attempt suicide either."

Ms. Reynolds and Dr. Winthrop exchange glances.

"I'm doing everything I'm supposed to be doing here. This is my fourth day. Can't I go home? Please? I'm being really good."

Ms. Reynolds jots something down and then asks, "Are you going to continue to cope with harmful behavior? Our goal is for you to stop hurting yourself."

You can't argue that you didn't "hurt" yourself because you did do damage to yourself, although it didn't hurt. "You're right. I did hurt myself. I admit that. It was stupid of me to *mess around* with safety pins. But that was all it was. There's no way I could have killed myself with safety pins. Really! And no. I'm not going to do that anymore."

You look at your parents and say, "Mom, Dad, I promise. I'm not going to do anything stupid like that anymore. Ever, ever again."

Shayna speaks. "She's working very hard in therapy through Healthy Foundations, and she's on target with other girls in her group in terms of participation and determination."

Thank you, Shayna.

Again, Ms. Reynolds jots something down.

Damian says, "From everything I've seen while on duty, she's an exemplary patient."

Thank you, Damian.

Dr. Winthrop turns her attention to Janet. "And how is she doing with her medication?"

"Well, she was on Zoloft but she stopped taking it before she was admitted," Janet replies.

Everyone looks from Janet to you.

"I stopped taking my pills about four weeks ago. I told Janet that," you say. You want to be as agreeable as possible so they'll let you go home.

"I've called her primary doctor and left two messages, which have not been returned. I need to confirm with him how many milligrams before we put her back on Zoloft," Janet says.

Dr. Winthrop addresses your parents: "Do you think your daughter needs to be on an antidepressant and were you aware she stopped taking her meds?"

Your mom speaks. "I recently found out she stopped taking her pills, but I thought you put her back on Zoloft once she was admitted. She was on one hundred milligrams and seemed to be doing well on that. I thought so anyway. Lately, she's been so unhappy."

"Well, yes," Dr. Winthrop says. "The cutting could have been because she went off her meds." She writes something down and then looks at Janet. "You should have told me immediately that you couldn't get in touch with her primary. I can prescribe her one hundred milligrams of Zoloft. She should have started the medication the day she arrived."

You're hoping the next thing she says will be that she'll let you go home with your parents after she writes you up a new prescription.

But that's not what Dr. Winthrop says.

"Very well. We've scheduled discharge in four days, so we'll shoot for Tuesday afternoon. Since it's Friday, things are a little slow over the weekend with therapists' availability. She'll get limited therapy sessions over the weekend, but we think therapy on Monday and Tuesday will be beneficial. We want to make certain she's ready to go home."

You feel the tears come and you can't control them. You wonder if anyone understands that you've got an eating disorder, that you don't belong here, and you're not in danger of killing yourself. You look around the room and you see that there might be two people who do understand that you being here is a huge mistake—Damian and Shayna. The two of them look shocked to hear that you'll be staying another four days.

"Are you sure that's necessary? Another four days?" Shayna asks. "She's getting all the therapy she needs at Healthy Foundations."

Dr. Winthrop nods curtly. "We're sure, we're very sure. It's best that she stays here under our supervision. The good news is we have a flexible visitors' schedule over the weekend. You'll be able to spend more time with your parents than just an hour each night."

You turn to your mom and dad, tears streaming down your face. "Mom, Dad? Do I have to stay?"

Your mom and dad look at each other and then your mom says, "We were hoping you could come home too, but if Dr. Winthrop thinks you should stay for a few more days then you probably should."

You have never felt so defeated in all your life.

55

After the meeting, Dr. Winthrop suggests you go to your room until therapy so that you can calm down. She feels a rest will do you some good.

In your room, you slide your hand under the thin mattress where you put Ben's letter. You want to read his words; they'll reassure you someone cares for you, that someone wants you. But when you reach for the letter, you can't feel it. You thought you had shoved it up high, but maybe it's farther down, so you move your hands lower. When you can't feel the crisp paper, you get on your knees on the hard floor and lift the mattress, getting a bit frenzied.

It's not there.

You lie flat on the floor and scan under the bed.

Nothing.

Your heart is pumping wildly and you begin to tear the room apart, pulling your pillowcase off the pillow, removing the sheets, yanking the scratchy blanket all the way down to the floor. You're crying and yelling, "It's not here! It's not here!"

You're hysterical.

It's all you have of Ben.

You open the dresser drawers, then bang them shut, and then tear the other bed apart–Savara's bed–knowing your letter is not going to be there either, because you know, *you know*, the letter was under your mattress and now it's not in your room.

Minutes later you sense a presence in the doorway.

Ken.

You know then that he's taken your letter.

"You looking for something?" he sneers.

You wipe your nose and push your hair away from your splotchy face.

"You give it back, you asshole."

He turns from the doorway and begins to walk away. Before you know what you're doing, you slam your body into his and beat your fists into his back. You scream at him, "Give it back! Give it back!" and, "You're an asshole and a thief! You thief!" You pound at his flesh and he turns toward you like he's going to hit you and the next thing you know you've knocked Ken's glasses from his face and you scratch at him with all the energy you have. Your fingernails slide against his cheek and he lets out a howl.

Two guards come and grab your arms to pull you away from Ken.

"The chick's crazy," Ken yells, grabbing his face. "She freaking attacked me!"

"He's a thief! He stole my letter! He went into my room and went through my things!" you yell.

Dr. Winthrop and Damian come around the corner to see what all the commotion is and when Dr. Winthrop sees your room has been ransacked, she asks, "What's going on?" She looks at you and Ken, and sees that Ken has a bloody scratch on his face.

"She attacked me!" Ken accuses.

"He went through my room!" you say.

"Did you do that to her room?" Dr. Winthrop asks Ken.

"No, I just stopped by to see if she wanted to play cards or checkers. I was bored. And she freaked out on me!"

"You're a liar!" you yell.

"Who did this to your room?" Dr. Winthrop asks you.

You're silent.

"Who did it?" she asks again.

"I did," you say. "I was looking for a letter of mine."

"Did you do that to his face?" Dr. Winthrop asks you.

You're silent.

"Are you not going to speak?" she asks.

You remain silent. Ken smirks from the hallway.

Dr. Winthrop is fuming. "I warned you last time, did I not? And violence? We do *not* tolerate violence in here. Damian, take Ken to Janet to have those scratches looked at."

Then Dr. Winthrop stares at you with hate in her eyes.

"You. Come with me."

* * *

You're in a room alone, with just a bed and a toilet in the far corner. Dr. Winthrop put you here so you can think about whether or not you want to tell her why you felt compelled to become so violent, when she has been "so very good to you. And you were so close to being discharged."

The walls are white, the bedsheet is white. Besides the bed and the toilet there is nothing else in the room. You wonder if Winthrop will keep you here for the next four days. Or longer now? Your parents will kill Winthrop if they find out what she's doing to you, because being locked up like this isn't therapy, this is abuse. You're emotionally exhausted and you can't believe this is happening.

This is your fucked-up life.

And it all began because you can't eat some foods.

All because of a stupid-ass monster who lives inside you.

All because someone sent an anonymous e-mail and you got sent to the Crazy House.

You have no idea what time it is but Winthrop locked you up around three-thirty. Someone brought you a snack but of course you don't eat it because you *have an eating disorder but they don't get that because they think you are suicidal.*

You're on the bed staring at the ceiling when there is a quick tap on the door and it opens. It's Winthrop. She enters the room and stares down at you.

"Well?" she asks.

When you don't say anything, she continues. "I just spoke to Ken at dinner and he says that he did nothing to provoke you."

"He's at dinner? He's not locked up? Why am I in here but he's not in trouble?"

"You were the violent one. Did you see what you did to his face?"

"He's a thief! He's not in any trouble? He went through my room. He stole from me!"

"What did he take?"

"A letter from my boyfriend."

"And that's a reason to scratch his face up? Do you see now why we think you need to stay here? You have severe anger issues, you're dangerous not only to yourself but to others as well. We were right to suggest you stay longer."

You have no fight left in you so you close your eyes, signifying that you're done with the conversation. She's not going to listen to anything you have to say anyway. She's been against you since you arrived and nothing's going to change her mind.

"I came here to give you a chance to come to dinner, but you're not cooperating. I believe this conversation is over." And she leaves.

A while later a horrible plate of food is delivered. You eat the roll and drink the warm carton of milk and your gag reflex hits and you almost throw up. You try to keep down the bread and the milk but the thought of curdled milk being churned in your stomach is unsettling and you throw up anyway. You don't make it to the toilet and the vomit hits the linoleum floor with an unsavory splat. Since the only thing you could clean it up with would be the bedsheet, you leave the mess on the floor. The smell is horrendous and it saturates the room.

You crawl back onto the bed and get as close to the wall as you can, curl into the fetal position and pull the cold sheet over your body. That's all there is, one cold white starched sheet. Not even a blanket to keep you warm.

You cry.

And you cry. And you cry. Harder than you've ever cried in your life.

Fuck this monster. You've never hated anything more. You hate what's happening to you. You need to fix this. You thought you were on your way. Dr. Winthrop is crazy. You don't know what you're going to do. You're trapped. It's no wonder Malik killed himself. It was his only way out. His only way out of this Crazy House.

There is no hope at all.

You close your eyes and wish for death. This is the only way you think you'll get out of this place.

Then because there is nothing else to do, you start screaming.

You scream and scream and scream until everything goes black.

Your hair is matted to your face and your throat feels like razors slashed every part of it from all the screaming. No one came for you, and as far as you know, no one checked on you during the night. Now though, you hear commotion from the other side of the door, and it's getting louder.

"What's that horrible smell?" You hear angry voices, and then the door opens and your parents rush in. "Christ! Get my daughter out of here!" your dad demands. "This is bullshit!"

Your mom comes over to the bed and pulls you to her. She hugs you tight and you start crying all over again.

"Honey, it's okay, it's okay. We're so sorry, I'm so sorry. You're coming home. Right now. Right now, baby. We're taking you home."

When you get into your parents' car, the first thing you do is ask your mom for your phone back. You text Ben to tell him that you'll be home in about an hour. The next thing you do is leave a message for Shayna to let her know that your parents have taken you out of the hospital and hopefully you will see her at Healthy Foundations this week.

Then your mom tells you how they discovered you.

"We decided to take advantage of the Saturday-morning visiting hours."

She turns to face you in the backseat. "We felt awful about how we left you yesterday," your mom says. "We knew how upset you were and we felt so bad."

"When we arrived," your dad continues, "Dr. Winthrop wasn't there. When no one could tell us where you were, when you weren't in your room, then I knew for sure something was wrong."

You sink back into the seat with such relief to be going home. The only regret you have is you left the Crazy House so quickly you didn't get to say goodbye to Chad or Damian. You feel like they were both looking out for you, that they genuinely cared about you, and now you'll never see them again.

You are so glad to be out of there you want to cry again, but good tears. You can't believe the types of emotions you have experienced in the past four days. And when you pull up to your house, there's another emotion you get to experience because Ben is standing in your driveway with a bunch of white carnations in his hands and a huge smile on his face.

Waiting for you.

Just as he said he would be.

56

Before the car comes to a complete stop you open the door, stumble out, and you're in Ben's arms, hugging him. You smell him and he kisses your hair and inhales you. You hope he can't smell the stale milk and vomit on you, then you realize he doesn't care, he only cares about you. About being with you.

You smell flowers and Ben. You inhale deeply, wanting to commit the smell to memory. It's wonderful. It's hopeful. You're home.

"Ben, you're here?" your mom asks as she gets out of the car, and you think she's being rude. Your dad is by the trunk gathering your things.

"I wanted to come over right away." He's looking down at you, into your eyes, and he pushes your unwashed hair away from your face. You want to look at him forever.

"Well, she's going to need a shower and probably a long nap. Maybe it would be better if you came back tomorrow, don't you think?" your mother asks.

"Mom!" you croak. Your throat still aches from the scream-ing. "I haven't seen him in almost a week. Let him stay. I'll shower really quick, and then we'll go get something to eat. I promise I'll go eat something healthy. I'll eat a salad. I will!" You're begging your mother for this.

"Ben," your dad interrupts. "We think Pea needs some rest. So why don't you head back home and she'll call you when she's had a bit of a rest. How 'bout it, buddy?"

Ben's face falls, but he's not one to argue with adults—he's respectful and kind—you know that, and that's just one of the many reasons you love him. But you can't believe your parents are going to send him away, after all you've been through.

"You can't make him leave!" you yell. "Don't you guys know what I've just been through? This is crap!"

"Pea." Your dad sounds threatening.

"Hey," Ben says quietly to you. "I'll call you later, okay?" He pushes the hair away from your ear and whispers, "I love you." Then to your parents he says, "See you later, Mr. Richards, Mrs. Richards."

He hands you the bouquet of carnations, gets into his car, and gives you a slow wave goodbye.

You turn to your parents and say, "I don't know why you're doing this. Why did you make him leave—why can't I see him?"

"We just think you need to slow things down a bit," your mom says. "You need to rest. You must be exhausted and it's been a horrible week for you."

You're fuming, but Ben's already gone so there's no point in arguing. You turn and storm into the house and wonder if you just went from one Crazy House to another Crazy House.

After you take a shower, you get into bed and do a quick scroll through Twitter and Instagram. There's no way you're going downstairs to talk to your parents. You can't believe they sent Ben home. You send Jae a text and she texts you back immediately.

I'm home.

OMG I FREAKED WHEN YOUR MOM TOLD ME EVERY-THING. I'M COMING OVER!

I don't know if you can. My parents sent Ben home.

WTF?

ikr

Well, I'm coming over in a little while!

k

You take a long nap and it feels luxurious. When there's a knock on the door later, you figure it's your mom checking on you.

"What?"

The knob turns and Jae bounces in and plops onto your bed, flopping into you, giving you a half hug. "I missed you!"

"Missed you too." You hug her back. "You got past the wardens?"

"They didn't even search me," Jae says, laughing. "Your voice! It's wrecked!"

"Yeah, I did a little screaming while I was there."

"Oh my God!" Jae says, and then, "Can I see your wrists?"

You show them to her and say, "See, it's not even a big deal."

Jae holds your wrists and looks at your skin, turns your palms over.

"It's not that bad. But, you weren't, I mean, I know you, you wouldn't . . . Are you really okay?" Jae squeezes your hands tightly and you squeeze back.

"Jae. I wouldn't do anything like that. Ever. Things have been tough, but the intention was never there."

Jae lets go of your hands, hugs you quickly one more time, and then releases you.

"Why aren't they letting you see Ben?" she asks.

"I have no fricking clue. He didn't do anything wrong. They're pissing me off so much."

"So what was it like, was it awful?"

"Pretty much." You pull yourself up on the bed, then flip over and put your legs up the side of the wall. "Actually the only good thing was the other kids there, and one of the staff members, Damian."

You tell Jae about your mortifying exam from the nurse and then you tell her how cool Damian was, how he brought you your love letter from Ben, and then how asshole Ken stole it, and how after you scratched up his face, you got thrown into solitary confinement, where you spent all last night screaming.

"Wow," Jae says. "It just sounds so bad. And you, in solitary for beating up a guy? Pretty badass, though."

"I guess so." You shrug.

You talk about Starling and Savara and Chad, how Chad was intense and interesting and hard to understand, how Savara was someone that you might not have ever talked to in your entire life but you really got to know her and probably would consider her a friend if you spent more time together. You tell her about poor Malik, and you feel weepy over it.

"It just sucked," you admit. "They don't have any clue how to treat kids or deal with what's going on with them. They didn't know how to deal with our emotions. It sucked."

Jae is thoughtful for a moment and then she says, "I'm really sorry."

"Me too."

"Did it help at all?"

You consider her question. On the one hand, not really. But on the other hand, you know you never want to go back. And you also realize that only you have the power to get rid of the monster. No one else can do it for you. No therapists. No doctors. No parents.

Only you can do this.

And you want it more than anything. You want to be free

of the monster, free of the feelings he invokes in you. Free, so you can have a better life, a good life, and be able to do the things normal girls can do, and be free from the constraining feelings you have all the time. You don't want to be restricted in your life any longer. So maybe that's what you learned by being stuck in the Crazy House.

Jae asks you again, "So did it help?"

"Maybe a little, maybe a little bit." Then you are both quiet for a while, lying on your bed like you always do, almost like things are normal again. Jae's playing with her split ends, and you're drawing circles with your toes on the wall.

57

You have to see Ben today, but there's no way your parents are going to let you, so you and Jae come up with a plan. As Jae's leaving, you ask your mom if the two of you can go to a movie later.

"Please, Mom, I've been locked up for almost a week. I need to get out," you say.

She hesitates for a moment but then Jae says, "Come on, Mrs. Richards, I haven't seen her all week. Please?"

"Only if you have her home by ten-thirty."

"Promise!" Jae says to your mom. And to you, she says, "I'll pick you up at seven!"

Your mom doesn't see Jae wink at you. Neither does your dad because he's glued to the TV.

After Jae leaves, you go into the kitchen and open the fridge. You're going to start killing the monster. The first part of the plan is to eat. You're desperate to try as you look at the contents of the refrigerator. There's Greek yogurt, and eggs, and cheese, milk, apples, carrot sticks, ketchup, mustard, some leftover stuff in Tupperware containers you're not ready to open, but maybe you'll get there someday. There is some packaged lettuce and you decide you can try a salad. That sounds safe. It will also show your parents you are trying.

You pull out the lettuce and put some into a bowl, and since you know croutons are safe, and you also like carrot sticks, you put some of those into the bowl too. Your mom comes over to you and hugs you tight, almost smothering you.

"Are you doing okay, honey? Can I do anything for you?"

"I'm okay, Mom," you say.

"We're glad you're home, Pea," your dad says from the family room, ESPN blaring in the background.

"I'm happy that you're trying," your mom says, nodding encouragingly toward your salad. "Can I get you anything else?" You can tell she's treading lightly and she wants to help you. You know she spoke with Shayna a couple of times when you were in the hospital, so maybe she's trying some skills of her own.

You don't know where Todd is. You haven't seen him since you got home from the hospital and you think that's *really* nice of him. It's like he didn't even care you were gone four full days. *Whatever,* you think. He's out of your life in less than a year anyway, hopefully, if he goes away to college. Then you won't have to deal with him or his lack of sympathy ever again.

Dad's watching his sports show and Mom's hovering a little too much. Now, it's battle time between you and the monster.

You're going to eat this salad—this lettuce and croutons and carrots—and you'll drown the monster in some vegetables. Then you'll go back upstairs to figure out what's next.

You feel proud, and empowered by your plan.

At the kitchen counter you eat the salad. You take your time, and are thoughtful in your chewing, and you silently say, *Die, monster*, with every bite. You crunch the croutons and carrots, and manage to eat everything in the bowl. When you're done with it, you put your bowl in the sink and your mom looks at you from the kitchen table, where she was trying not to hover. She smiles.

"Am I going back to Healthy Foundations on Monday?" you ask.

"Yes," your mom says. "That's the plan."

"Good. I like Shayna. I need her. I think that was working."

"I'm so proud of you, honey. I'm sorry if I haven't told you that enough."

"Thank you, Mom."

"I love you," she says.

"I love you too," you say. "I'm going to go upstairs and get ready for the movie."

When you get upstairs, you text Ben:

> Hey
>
> Hey what are you doing?
>
> Just ate some stuff that tasted like grass

What?

Salad

Oh good. You don't like that though

I'm trying

can I come over?

Yes. But my parents are being weird

I know. why?

No idea, worried about me. They're dumb. Come over anyway.

You sure? I don't want you to get in trouble.

Seriously. Are they gonna ground me? They already threw me into the Crazy House. Besides I told them I'm going to the movies with Jae. Come at 7 but don't come to the door. I'll meet you outside.

OK

XO

XO

You pull on your Chucks and go downstairs. Your brother has appeared and is on the couch with his earbuds in, texting someone. He gives you a sideways glance and says, "Hey, you're home," like it was no big deal that you were in a psych ward for four days. You completely ignore him. If he acts this way to you when you've been going through this much–like you don't exist in his world–then screw him.

You kiss your mom and dad and tell them you'll wait for Jae outside.

"Be home by ten-thirty," your mom says.

"Where's she going?" Todd asks.

"What do you care?" you snip.

"She's going to a movie with Jae," your dad says. You're shocked that he was paying attention.

"Bye!" you say. You can't wait to get out of here. You've definitely traded one Crazy House for another.

Outside, you wait on the curb and when you see Ben's car you stand up fast, not wanting your parents to see that he's picking you up. When he pulls up you open the passenger door and jump into his car.

"Hi," you say.

"Hey." He reaches over to you, puts one hand behind your neck, pulls you to him, and kisses you hard on the mouth. You kiss him back fiercely. You can't stand the fact that you missed him this much. "Where can we go? I just want to be with you."

He kisses you some more, puts his hands on either side of your face and looks at you deeply. "Where do you want to go?"

"Anywhere we can be alone and you can just hold me. We have until ten-thirty."

Ben drives to Lone Dog Mountain, the place of your first kiss, where you tried to search for shooting stars but the only stars you saw that night were the ones floating in each other's eyes. He holds your hand the whole way there, and there's no music on and you don't talk, and that's completely okay. You're not sure how you're feeling, but you're definitely filled with all sorts of emotions because you don't know what's going to happen. You're with the boy you love and you're not sure what you might want to do next. The only thing you know for certain is that you want to be with him.

When you get to the trailhead, he parks in the empty parking lot but you don't get out. He turns off the ignition and looks at you. You swallow hard. You inhale. He pulls you to him and you're kissing again, the kind of kissing that makes your stomach flop all over the place, way down deep, the kissing that makes you think you might want to do other things.

"Do you want to get in the back of the car?" he whispers warm in your ear, then keeps kissing you. His words heat your body, they burn through you.

You don't stop kissing but you nod yes. He's still kissing you and he holds on to your body while your arms are tightly wound around his neck. He uses his strength to maneuver the two of you to the back of the SUV. You hadn't noticed before but the backseats are already down.

"My dad and I moved a dresser today, that's why the seats are down," he explains.

Ben gently places you on the lowered seat and positions himself along your side, and stops kissing you for a moment. He caresses your cheek, then kisses your forehead.

"I have to tell you something," he says.

"What is it?" you ask.

"It's really important," he says. "I don't want you to be angry with me."

"Ben, tell me. Nothing you can say will make me angry."

"I sent in that anonymous tip to your school."

You freeze.

You feel as if you can't move. Your body goes cold and your limbs go numb. Fear pumps through you. This is wrong.

He keeps talking. "I had no idea they would send you away, or I would never have done it."

"You what? *You what?*"

Your eyes have gone wide. You feel the shock all the way through to your toes. He's still holding you, still touching you.

"I care about you so much," he says.

"When? When did you do it?"

"The night I first saw the cuts. When I brought you to my house. I didn't want you to kill yourself. I was so scared. I didn't know what else to do. I guess I could have called your parents but I wasn't thinking straight. I don't know. You told me not to tell them. I should have told my mom—that probably would have been the best thing to do. I thought you might really do something dangerous. I've never dealt with anything like that. The marks on your hands and wrists . . . I've never had anyone I've cared about hurt themselves."

You're still numb, but you're listening to him.

"Then, Saturday, I thought I shouldn't have done it so I e-mailed another note saying it might not have been as bad as

I thought. But once you send in a tip like that, they're going to take it seriously. And when we were together on Sunday at the lake, things didn't seem so bad in the daylight, and you promised me you wouldn't do it again. I believed you. I'm so sorry. It was me who put you in that horrible place."

He lowers his head against your shoulder and you know how distraught he is over this.

"I thought a girl from my class sent it in. Or Alex," you whisper. "I thought he might have seen me do it ..."

He looks up at you. "No, it was me."

You think about it. You really think about it and you finally get it.

You know why he did it, and you soften.

You understand.

Ben didn't do it for any other reason than he thought he was doing the right thing. He had no idea where you would end up.

He touches your hair, your eyelashes. He's sad, and you know he wants so badly for you to forgive him.

"I didn't want them to take you away. But I want you to get better."

You believe him. You've never believed anyone's words more.

"I'm sorry, I'm so sorry for what I put you through," he says. "I love you."

"I know. It's okay. It's okay. I love you too." You do. You love him and you've never wanted to be with him more than at this moment. You press your lips to his again and you kiss for a long while, your tongues intertwined. You taste peppermint. You suck his tongue, then bite his lower lip. He groans.

All you want to do is be with him.

Your Ben.

He pulls you closer.

"Are we okay? Are you okay?" he whispers.

You nod that you're okay. Everything is okay.

You want him to touch you. You want to feel his skin against yours. You run your hands under his shirt and feel his strong chest, his shoulders, his forearms. His fingers reach under your shirt and lightly graze the fabric of your bra, and then his palms are over the tops of your bra cups, squeezing gently. You feel your body ignite like it never has before. The heat is intense.

"Should we take our shirts off?" he whispers.

"Yeah."

You both sit up and he pulls his shirt off quickly and tosses it to the floor. You press your palms against his smooth chest. His skin is warm and you feel his heart beating all the way through to your fingertips.

He lifts your shirt from your arms and removes it from your shoulders and over your head, but he doesn't take your bra off. You don't know what you should do, if you should take your bra off or not. So you wait.

Ben looks at you.

Although it's dark out, there's enough glow from the moon that he can see you.

You know that on the first day you met, and just under a week ago at the lake, he saw you in less clothing than you have on now, but this, this is different.

The boy you love is still looking at you.

You don't know what to do with your hands, and you feel exposed. You don't want to feel this way with someone you love so much. But then Ben takes his hands and places them on your shoulders and moves them up and down slowly along the sides of your arms, as if to warm you. He looks into your eyes, not at your chest, not greedily, just like a boy who loves you for who you are.

"I'm so sorry for everything," he says.

He places his hand over your heart.

Your heart is thumping louder than it ever has before. It might explode.

"I do love you, so much, you know that," he says.

"I know."

He kisses you and you know for certain that this is real.

He lowers you back down onto the seat and you kiss some more, and now you are practically skin to skin. It feels so good, his warm body covering your body, this is absolutely perfect and right. You are safe and bathed in the moon's glow. You know that Ben has always had your best interests at heart.

From the very first day you met.

So you kiss and you kiss and he touches you softly and you let him do this. He kisses your skin all over and you kiss his chest and his neck and his arms. You touch each other, memorizing the moments, his breath, this night. You are learning about each other and loving each other, and there's absolutely, positively nothing wrong with that.

It's all completely beautiful.

Ben is beautiful.

The two of you together are beautiful.

58

You pull up to your house and Ben barely has a chance to put his car into Park when you see a shadow at his door. It flies open and someone pulls him out of the driver's seat. It's your brother, and he's shouting and grabbing at Ben.

It happens so fast, you aren't sure what's going on but there's yelling and punching and you jump out of the car and start screaming at Todd to stop and you try to pull Todd from Ben but not before he gets a good punch to Ben's face.

"Stay away from my sister, you asshole!"

Then there's blood spurting from Ben's nose and Todd grabs you by the forearm, hard.

"Come with me!" he yells, and pulls you toward the house.

Ben is bent over, holding his nose, and blood is pouring from his face and you're crying and screaming at Todd as he drags you away.

"What the fuck! What are you doing? Ben! Ben!"

The front light comes on and your parents rush out to the

porch. Your mom is wearing green silk lounge pants and a sleep T-shirt, and she's holding a half-empty glass of wine. Your dad looks like he has been sleeping in front of the TV, and his hair is sticking up all over the place.

"What's going on out here!" your dad shouts.

"Ben came and got her. She didn't go out with Jae to a movie!" Todd accuses.

Your dad glares at you.

"Pea, get in the house," he orders. "Now."

You turn to look at Ben, and now you're crying uncontrollably. Ben has taken his shirt off and holds it up to his nose to try to stop the bleeding. The shirt has turned bright red with his blood.

"Don't you touch me ever again!" you scream at Todd as you rip his hold from your arm. "I hate you!"

You rush past your parents and as you do, you say to them, "I hate you both too. I hate this whole fucking family."

You lock yourself in your room and think about what you're going to do. There's no way you're staying here with these crazies. *No way*, you think. You can't believe your brother, your fucking brother, who never says two words to you, who hasn't even acted like he cared about you in the past God knows how many years, just beat up your boyfriend. For what reason? To show off? It's not like he loves you. He totally doesn't.

You're livid and you need to get away from your family. And you need to make sure Ben is okay.

You heard Ben drive off when you ran into the house and you hope he went straight to the hospital because you're pretty sure Todd broke his nose. You send a text to him and then you throw some clothes into an overnight bag and text Jae:

I need ur help. Come get me now. Emergency!

On my way!

Someone knocks on your door but you scream from the other side, "Don't! I'm not coming out, so don't try to talk to me!"

"Honey, please," your mom says.

"No!"

She tries again to talk to you and then you hear your dad's voice outside your room too.

"Pea, we've got to talk about this."

"I'm not talking to anyone right now," you shout back. "I'm going to sleep. Maybe I'll talk to you both tomorrow!"

After a few more attempts to get you to open your door, your parents give up and you hear them walk down the stairs.

When Jae texts you that she's at your house you sneak out your bedroom window like you did the last time, and you don't care if you get caught. Because fuck it, look what your brother did to your boyfriend, and your parents just had you holed up in a psych ward for almost a week, so what's the worst that can happen? You do decide to text your parents to let them know you're going to stay at Jae's, that you need some space and some time to think. You don't say it nicely though, but you'll deal with them later.

You hop into Jae's car and she hugs you hard. You fight back tears when you tell her what happened. She drives you to the hospital, because Ben texted you that that's where he went. When you arrive, Jae drops you at Emergency while she parks. You rush in and see Ben's mom.

"Honey, Ben told me you were coming. He wanted me to make sure to find you," Mrs. Hansworth says as she hugs you.

The tears come.

Why can't your mom be more like her, you think.

"Is he okay?" you ask.

"Broken nose, split lip," Mrs. Hansworth says.

"My brother did it to him. I have no idea why," you say between tears.

She hugs you again and rubs your back. "He'll be okay. Families can do crazy things, you know. He wants to see you though."

"Can I?"

"Yes, through those double doors and second curtain on the right."

"My friend Jae is parking her car, she's got a blue hoodie on..."

"I'll tell her where you are when she comes in."

"Thank you."

"Go," Mrs. Hansworth says, and points to the doors.

When you get to the room, you pull the curtain and try not to look shocked. Ben's face is not too pretty. His nose, his beautiful nose is lopsided on his face, and even though they cleaned up all the blood, there is still redness and swelling and bruises are forming underneath his eyes. You take a tentative step toward the bed.

"Hey," you say.

"Not quite the way our night was supposed to end, huh?" He attempts to lift his lips into a smile but he grimaces and moves his hand to his face.

"Hurts bad?" you ask.

"Kind of."

"I can't believe...I just...I'm so..." You bite your bottom lip to keep it from quivering.

"Don't say it. None of this is your fault. Your brother's just... Well, I might not even say he's a total asshole. You know, I have little sisters. So I might be protective of them too."

"What?"

"He's worried about you."

You sit on the edge of the hospital bed and look at his face.

"You got stitches too?" you ask, when you see dark threaded lines crisscrossing the corner of his mouth.

"Just three."

"But on your lip?"

"You can kiss it and make me feel better," Ben says.

You lean toward him and look closer at his gorgeous face, the face of the boy who loves you.

You touch his lips lightly with yours, just soft enough, just carefully enough so that you don't hurt him.

You don't pull away, you are still lips to lips, but you ask, "Is that better?"

"It's perfect," he says. "You're perfect."

59

When you open the doors to go back to the waiting room you're surprised to see your dad standing there, hands in his pockets, with a concerned look on his face. You're expecting him to be pissed at you for basically running away from home, but then he reaches his arms out to you.

You run to him and he puts his arms around you and you begin to sob like a seven-year-old who just fell off her bike and tore open her knees.

"It's okay, Pea. Everything will be okay. I promise."

"Dad, Todd beat him up."

He holds you while you cry. It's soothing and also strange, this feeling of your dad holding you, protecting you, taking care of you. It's been so long since he's shown affection toward you, you don't know what to make of it.

But it feels really comforting.

When you're finished crying, you wipe your nose on your dad's sleeve and you both sort of laugh at the weirdness of it all.

"How's he doing?"

"I think he hurts pretty bad."

"How are you doing?" your dad asks you.

"Not too good." You see that Jae showed up and is sitting with Ben's mom.

"I just wanted to make sure that you were okay. Your mom and I are so worried about you. She stayed home in case you decided to come back. I first went to Jae's house and her parents told me I'd find you here. I just needed to make sure you were okay."

You try to hold in your tears but you begin to whimper. When you think of everything that you've been through, and now Ben being hurt, it's just too much to take.

"I'm so sorry, honey, that you're dealing with all this," your dad says to you. "I know I'm not the best at this emotional stuff."

"Thanks, Dad." It's what you needed to hear from your father and you hug him again and smile. Your dad is doing exactly what you need him to do.

Ben's mom comes over then. Your dad says they talked while you were in with Ben, and even though you know Mrs. Hansworth would never be mean, it feels weird to think that your boyfriend's mother is talking to the dad of the guy who beat him up.

Your dad continues to apologize for what Todd did and tells Mrs. Hansworth that he will be punished. While they talk, you go sit by Jae.

"This is some effed-up shit," Jae says. She asks if you're going home with your dad.

"No way. I mean, it's great that he came to the hospital and all, but I can't deal with being at home right now. And I definitely don't want to see Todd."

When your dad and Mrs. Hansworth are done talking, they come over to you and Jae and you ask your dad if you can still stay with Jae and he says yes.

"Mrs. Hansworth, can I say bye to Ben really quick?" He looked so banged up in there, and you need to see him one more time before you leave for the night.

"I don't see why not, just check with the nurse first."

You say goodbye to your dad and even give him one more hug, then check with the nurse and she says you can see Ben. You feel so much better now than you did when you first got to the hospital. It seems like there was a small breakthrough with your dad. It felt weird but also real, for the first time in a long while, like chipping away at a huge, solid ice block. You think that ice eventually has to melt. You're glad your dad came to the hospital, and relieved that Mrs. Hansworth doesn't hate him.

When you get to Ben's room, you pull the curtain and see that he's sleeping. You move to the bed and watch his chest rise and fall.

You can't believe he's a part of your life.

You can't believe he loves you so much.

You can't believe your brother beat him up.

You can't believe this is your crazy life.

But it is.

You don't want to wake him and you wish more than anything that you could curl up next to him, to be here when he wakes up, to tell him once again that you love him and you're so sorry your brother did this. But you'll tell him all of this later, and so much more. You want to tell him everything you think of.

You want to tell him every thought you have.

You move a bit closer and search his sleeping face. His eyelids flutter but don't open. His eyelashes—how could you never have noticed how long they are, how feathery light and perfect? You get close enough to see tiny sprinkles of veins in his eyelids and you're certain he can feel your breath on his face, even though he is sound asleep.

You don't want to wake this boy you love.

You kiss one eyelid and then the other.

"I love you, Ben. I love you."

60

You wake Sunday morning alone in Jae's room. You feel like you slept for sixteen hours straight. It seems like a lifetime since you slept so peacefully and you don't remember the last time you woke with such a clear head.

The first thing you do is call Ben to see how he's doing. His mother answers his phone, and you're instantly freaked out that something is wrong.

"Where's Ben? Is everything okay?" you ask.

"Everything's fine," Mrs. Hansworth says. "We got home from the hospital at two in the morning, and he's still sleeping. I'll tell him you called."

You thank her and hang up, grateful to know Ben is okay.

Next, you figure out your plan for going home to face your family. You've decided you want Shayna with you because you feel she's the only one who can mediate this mess. She's the only one who can make sense of the craziness of your family. So you call her and leave a message, telling her it's not an emergency but it is important.

When Shayna calls you back an hour later, she says she got your message from Friday and the one you left earlier.

"I'm sorry I didn't call you back yet. How come you got out of St. Joe's early?"

You tell her everything that has occurred since the assessment meeting—you can't believe how much has happened—Ken harassing you, Winthrop putting you in solitary, Ben getting beaten up, *by your brother.* It's all just too much.

You also tell Shayna that you're ready for the next step. You want to start trying foods. You tell her you also need her help to make your parents understand that you're going to be okay, and you'd like her to help set boundaries at home. Although you felt a sort of thawing happening with your dad at the hospital, you know there's a lot more involved than a hug and an *I'm sorry* from him to make things right.

You need Shayna for the work that you'll have to do—the eating, the mindful thinking, the coping skills, the work to lower your anxiety . . . everything else it will take to get better. You know you cannot do it alone.

"I'm ready now," you tell her. "If being at St. Joe's taught me anything, it's that I'm stronger than I thought I was and I want to try really hard to fight this. I'm at my best friend's house now but will you come with me to my house today? I can't face my parents and brother alone."

She reminds you that it's Sunday.

"Please, Shayna, I can't go home alone. I need you there."

"Tomorrow morning? We can go there together tomorrow. Early, though, seven a.m.?" she says.

"Okay."

"I'll come get you and we'll go talk to your family together."

"Thank you, Shayna, thank you."

You give Shayna Jae's address and hang up, then you call your parents. They put you on speaker and you tell them that tomorrow morning at seven you'll be home, with Shayna, to talk to everyone. You tell them that you're going to seriously work on getting well, but it's going to be on your terms.

Then you ask your parents, "What is it about Ben that you don't like?"

When your mom speaks, you can tell she's tearful. Maybe also a bit remorseful. "It's not that we don't like Ben . . . but, you changed when he started coming around."

"That's not true," you say.

"It is," she says.

"I got happy," you say.

"You were doing things out of character," your mom says.

"You started hurting yourself," your dad interjects.

"You stopped taking your pills," your mom says.

"Ben makes me happy," you say. "And he didn't change me. He and Jae are the only ones who understand me. You guys don't understand everything that I'm going through, everything I'm dealing with. I know I made some mistakes and I'm willing to admit to them, but we've all made mistakes."

You're being really open with your parents and you're not sure what to make of it. You guess it's a start. And it seems like they're listening to you.

Then you ask another important question: "Why did Todd beat him up? I hate him for that."

"Pea, you might not believe this, and you might never get it, maybe not until you're a parent," your dad says. "But Todd loves you. Siblings have strange ways of showing their love for each other. I'm in no way condoning what he did, at all. What he did was absolutely wrong, but he did it out of love for you. He thought he was protecting you."

You think about this for a while, and there is a lull on the phone. You know there's work ahead of you. There's work to be done for all of you, if you want to get to the point of being a functional, loving family. Everyone is out of sync. But you're willing. You think they're willing. They love you. They do. You're still totally pissed at Todd though.

But maybe their willingness is enough for now. It's going to have to be.

"Tell Todd if he cares about me at all he has to be there to-morrow morning," you say. "He has to skip his morning foot-ball practice. He owes me this."

Before you hang up you tell your parents you love them.

61

Shayna picks you up at Jae's Monday morning and gives you a huge hug when she sees you.

"I'm so glad you're here," you say to her.

"I'm glad to be here," she says.

In the car on the way to your house, you tell Shayna what you've come to understand.

"I don't think there's a monster."

"What do you mean?" she asks.

"I think I might have made him up, or maybe he was just my conscience?"

"Uh-huh," Shayna says, her eyes on the road.

"So this monster, that's been a part of me for so long, hasn't really been real. Like just a thing, an extension of my behavior."

You are certain that the monster didn't really exist. He was everything around you, surrounding you. He was anxiety. He was depression. He was your brother. He was your parents when they were aggravating you. He was how you *felt* when you were hungry, or angry, or sad. He was the food that was keeping you from living your life this whole time. You unconsciously created the monster, someone else to blame, because you didn't want to take on the responsibilities of fixing what was broken.

The monster was never real.

"I'm ready," you tell Shayna. "I'm going to take the responsibility to get well, and not blame something else for my problems."

Of course, you'll need Shayna's help, and with time, patience, and determination, you'll succeed. You're sure of it. There have been girls like you before who have gotten well. And you know there will be girls like you after.

"I am so proud of you. You get it," Shayna says. "This is a huge realization on your part, a big step, you know?"

You smile at her, feeling confident, knowing you're figuring things out, knowing you're going to get better, knowing you're on your way to recovery.

When you get home, your parents and Todd are waiting. You're actually surprised that Todd skipped his morning football practice to be here. You're not quite sure what you want to say to him or how you feel about him. Your mom and dad both hug you, super-hard, almost to the point of being annoying, and your mom starts crying a little.

You get emotional too, thinking about everything you've

been through since you were sent to St. Joe's . . . You should be exhausted.

You sigh.

You are exhausted.

You plop yourself onto the couch while your mom gets coffee for Shayna and your dad, and then everyone else joins you in the family room. You're curled up with a blanket just waiting to see what will happen.

Your mom sits right next to you and takes your hand in hers. She whispers, "I'm so glad you're home."

You squeeze her hand back.

Shayna starts talking, just like she does in group sessions.

"Thanks, everyone, for being here."

Todd actually rolls his eyes, but he doesn't have earbuds in, which is a first.

"Todd, why don't we start with you," Shayna says. "What are your thoughts on your sister and what's been going on?"

"She hasn't been acting like herself. This guy comes into her life and she gets all weird, sneaking around, cutting herself, and sure, I'm worried she's just gonna end up getting hurt."

"Why do you think that?" Shayna asks.

"Because guys are dicks, and Ben's no different."

You want to say Ben's not like that, he loves you, and Todd knows nothing about him. Shayna glances at you as if to say, *Let him talk,* so you don't say anything. You sit there while your mom holds your hand and rubs it like she's never going to let go. Then you blurt out, "What do you care anyway, Todd. You don't even care about me."

"The fuck I don't!"

Everyone stares at Todd.

"You're my little sister. I don't want anyone hurting you."

He's still sulking.

Then Shayna asks your parents, "Do you have a problem with Ben?"

Your parents look at each other. You can tell your mom's thinking of what she wants to say without hurting your feelings.

"She's obviously not well," your mom starts. "We think she needs to concentrate on getting better first, before she gets serious with anyone."

Your mom smiles at you as if you've got a terminal illness or something.

"Mom! Stop it." You pull your hand away from her and put some space between the two of you.

"Why can't she do both?" Shayna asks your mom. "Why can't she have a supportive boyfriend by her side *while* she's getting better, while she's going through the program and learning to use the tools we're providing her?"

Your dad shifts his position on the couch, leans forward, as if to take control of the situation. "We have nothing against Ben. Ben's okay. We like him. We don't want her sneaking out and lying to us."

Shayna turns to you. "If your parents allow you to see Ben,

you have to respect their rules. This is their home, and you're their daughter. And lying is nonnegotiable."

You nod.

"He's very nice," your mom says. "I just don't want you to get hurt, and you got hurt with Alex—you ended up in the hospital. We had to put you on medication! And with Ben—with Ben, you started cutting, and look, you ended up in the hospital too."

"Mom, Dad, you have to know something," you say.

"What is it?" your mom asks.

"Ben is the one who sent in the anonymous tip to school about the cutting," you say.

"Now I really hate him," Todd says.

"No, you idiot!" you snap. "He was trying to help me and he thought that was the best thing to do!"

Shayna interrupts. "Ben did what he thought was right. It's pretty obvious he wants what's best for her. He's nothing like Alex and he's not going to intentionally hurt her."

Your mom reaches for your hand again. She's got tears puddling in her eyes so you take her hand in yours. Her emotions are aggravating you, but she is your mom so you can't blame her for being the way she is.

"I guess it's okay for her to see Ben," your mom says.

Your dad nods in agreement.

"Okay," Shayna says. "So we all understand that there's to be no more lying or sneaking out, and the kids must respect your rules."

You and your parents nod. Your mom says, "We pulled her out of the hospital so fast she never got that prescription from Winthrop. We need to get her back on Zoloft too."

"Okay," Shayna says. "Schedule an appointment with her primary doctor for this week so he can write the prescription."

"I'll do that," your mom says.

"And we'll continue at Healthy Foundations next Monday with one-on-one and group therapy. Take this afternoon and evening off. I'd also like to suggest some family therapy as well. The five of us, Todd, including you, we can meet maybe every other week? How do you feel about that?" Shayna specifically looks at Todd when she asks this. When he doesn't say anything, she nudges him.

"Todd? Are you okay with some family sessions?"

"Whatever," he says, and shrugs. "If it'll help."

"It will," Shayna says.

"Okay," Todd agrees.

"I think it's a good idea," your mom says. "There's been a disconnect in this family for a long time. Maybe therapy will help all of us?"

"Yes," your dad says.

"Therapy's tough on everyone. It takes a lot out of the patient, and it's work," Shayna tells your family. "She's trying really hard, is open to exploring new foods, and *wants* to get better. She really does. Right there is half the battle. I'm so proud of her."

"We are too," your mom says.

"Hold up, I'm still concerned about the cutting," your dad says.

Shayna looks to you for the answer.

"No more, Dad. That was just some crazy stuff. I can't explain it. But I don't want to do it anymore. I promise."

Then Todd speaks. "How is Ben?"

"You broke his nose and gave him stitches in his lip."

"Ow," he says.

"Yeah, not good."

"You need to get over there and apologize to him *and* his parents," your dad says to Todd.

"I was only looking out for my sister," Todd says. "Because *I love you*," he adds, and scrunches up his face in a weird way like it pains him to say it.

It's the first time in practically forever those words have come from his mouth directed at you and you almost fall off the couch. You feel a smile spread across your face.

"You're still a jerk," you say back, but you grin stupidly at Todd. You feel like you hate him just a tiny bit less for that small gesture of love, even though you do think he's a complete asshole for beating up your boyfriend.

"By the way, Todd," your mother adds, "you'll be paying for that hospital bill."

Now your smile grows wider.

"So," Shayna says, "we're all good with the plan?"

"Yes," your mom says. "I'm so happy!" She actually sighs next to you. You can feel her tension melt. You realize now that this has been hard on your parents too.

You exhale and feel something inside you churn. It's not the monster, because the monster doesn't exist. He never existed. It's a feeling of exhilaration, of being settled, of knowing that you're heading in the right direction.

The direction of recovery.

62

"Come on, I'll drive you to school."

Shayna has gone, and you, Todd, and your parents are in the living room.

"What?" you ask.

"Let's go," Todd says. "I have to get to school. I missed this morning's practice and if I don't show up this afternoon, Coach won't let me play Friday night."

"All right," you say.

You weren't sure if you were ready to go back to school today but no sense in putting off the inevitable. You'll have to face everyone and any rumors that are swirling around eventually. Might as well be today.

You tell Todd you need a minute and you run upstairs to brush your hair and grab your backpack. When you get downstairs, your mom hands you a paper bag that she's put together.

"Lunch," she says.

"Thanks," you say.

In the car, Todd is quiet and so are you. You don't know what to say to him. You think he might be annoyed that he's being forced to go to family therapy.

"Hey, I'm sorry," he finally says.

You swallow hard and are not sure how to respond, but his words make you emotional.

"I know I haven't been the best brother, and what I did to Ben was really shitty. So I'm sorry." He pats you on the thigh, a gesture only a big brother could pull off.

You don't want to cry, but it means so much coming from him, to hear him say those words. You blink back tears, glance at him really quickly, and say, "Thanks."

You look out the window the rest of the way, feeling all sorts of relief.

Although you weren't out of school for long, people gossip, and you're sure there are rumors about a suicide attempt. Some kids stare at you in the hallway, whisper when you walk by. You hear someone say something about an eating disorder but you ignore the talk. The kids who start those rumors don't matter to you. There are a few kids who are sympathetic and they ask how you're doing.

You feel good about yourself and the path you're on. You have Shayna to help you, your parents are being great, your brother actually apologized to you, and you've got Jae and Ben to support you. At school, your goal is to get through your classes and avoid drama. Between last year and recent events, you've had enough drama for a lifetime.

But there's one last thing you have to do to put this all behind you.

In English class, the six-word memoirs hang on the wall. Because it was in this class that things fell apart, you need to make it right.

You ask the girl who sits next to you—the one who noticed you bleeding that day—if you can borrow a sheet of paper. She smiles at you and hands you one that she pulls from a spiral notebook.

"You doing okay?" she asks.

"So much better, thanks," you answer.

On the sheet of paper, you scrawl six quick words and before Mr. Owens starts class you go to his desk and ask if you may borrow some tape because you'd like to add your new six-word memoir to the wall.

"Sure," he says, and hands you a roll of tape. "We're glad you're back."

"Me too," you say.

You pass Alex and make serious eye contact with him and give him a smile. It's a genuine smile, one that conveys something like *I'm over it, let's be over it*. You're not sure if you'll want to talk to him someday, but smiling at him feels like the closing of a chapter that you needed to end a long time ago.

You take your new memoir and go to the wall where the others are hanging. There are some interesting ones, one about being a basketball player, another about dancing through life, even one about reaching for the stars.

You tape your memoir on the wall. Maybe it will help another girl realize that it can be true for her. Maybe it'll help someone who doesn't know how hard things can get. Maybe it will give another girl the strength she'll need to get through her own battle. Because you're sure there are others than just you who need help. You hope someone who needs it will read your words and believe them as fiercely as you do.

My eating disorder doesn't control me.

Ben picks you up that afternoon and you suggest a drive to Lone Dog Mountain. You're not in the mood to hang out at home, and you're pretty sure Ben's not up for seeing Todd.

At Lone Dog, Ben parks the car in the lot but neither of you moves to get out. You tell him about that morning's meeting with Shayna and your parents, and how Todd apologized to you, and how he wants to apologize to him as well. You tell him about plans for family therapy and that things feel better between you and your parents, and they're okay with the two of you being together. You tell him you feel the best you've felt in a very long while.

Ben smiles at your news and moves closer to you.

He puts his hands on your cheeks and says your name.

"I love you," he says.

"I love you back," you say.

You remember the first day you saw him, that day on the river. That day that you thought was a partially good day, that turned out to be an amazing day. The day you floated on the river with the perfect boy who, just by holding your hand, made you feel all sorts of incredible, way down to the bottom of your toes.

Ben still makes you feel this way.

You want more of those days where you're filled with warmth, laughter, and love. You know you'll experience them, because you're getting well, and you've surrounded yourself with people who care about you.

He kisses you, and just like that . . .

. . . you're floating . . .

. . . under sun-drenched skies and white clouds . . .

. . . back on a river . . .

. . . free of the monster . . .

. . . that never existed.

acknowledgments

I thought writing the ending was hard, but this, so much more.

Thank you to Adriann Ranta at Foundry Literary + Media, who unslushed and loved this book. Thank you also to all the great people at Wolf Literary. Thank you, Margaret Ferguson, Susan Dobinick, and the incredible team at FSG, for bringing *Sad Perfect* to life.

To Trish, who has saved me more often than she knows in times of writing despair. You are a friend and writer extraordinaire and will always be my BBFF, forever and ever. I love you, Swishy!

To my best author friends, who have encouraged me through early drafts and rough rejections: Jess Riley, Eileen Cook, Liz Fenton, Lisa Steinke, Amy Sprenger, Jenna McCarthy, and Tracey Garvis Graves. To Amy Hatvany, who told me once, "Remember it only takes the right pair of eyes." Thank you to my good friend and book supporter Crystal Patriarche, and everyone at BookSparks.

My Chicago author girls: I miss you all more than you

know. Thank you for your long-distance love and friendship. I wish more than anything I could hang with you all, talk about our love of books and writing, and do lunch—with wine! You know who you are—much love!

To the members of The Sweet Sixteens—thank you for your mentoring and support, especially to Shannon M. Parker, Marisa Reichardt, Kathleen Glasgow, and Julie Buxbaum. To the amazing Swanky Seventeen admins and crew, and especially to Sara Biren—there's no way I could have gotten through the final book stages without you all. Your friendship, support, and jokes sustained me.

Thank you to my dear friends Cathy Braner, Robyn O'Halloran, Lauren Byrd, Tara McCarver, and author J. Nathan for reading an early draft and offering insightful feedback.

Thank you to all the teens and readers who have read *Sad Perfect*. If you're struggling with an eating disorder, especially ARFID, please know you can get better. Social anxiety, depression, and eating disorders are such debilitating issues that affect the whole family, and my heart goes out to those of you who struggle.

For their writing inspiration: Judy Blume—my first ever author crush—for introducing me to the world of reading with *Blubber* in fifth grade. Because of you, I never stopped reading and writing. To Rainbow Rowell, who writes perfect books. I was a goner with *Attachments*. And to Emily Giffin—there are no words to express my sincere gratitude to you—for your books, your friendship, your kindness.

To Colleen and Tom Stein, my beloved mom and dad, for letting me be a nerdy bookworm when I was a kid. For always buying me books, for getting me that robin's-egg blue Smith Corona typewriter for my fourteenth birthday, and then buying me an electric typewriter for college. Also, Dad, thanks for always saying, "What are you doing, writing a book?" whenever I asked you a question. Because now I can say, "Yeah, I did!"

To my siblings, Stacy, Scott, and Seth. Because you are my sibs and I'd never hear the end of it if your names weren't included. I love you all. Please read my book. Or tell your friends to read my book!

The biggest thanks to everyone at Healthy Futures, especially Kim DiRé, Mia Elwood, Jeanne Phillips, and Ilene Smith. You helped my family through a very difficult time and I am forever, ever grateful for your love and care.

I have to thank the boy who held my daughter's hand as they floated down the river together that summer day. It was you who inspired the first chapter of *Sad Perfect*.

To my husband, Scott—my Day One—and my dear sons, AJ and Luke; thank you for always being proud of me, and for telling people, "My wife/mom is an author." I think you believed it before I ever did. Luke, thank you for telling me to change Dr Pepper to Sprite in chapter 7. You are my guys and I love you all.

And finally, to my daughter, my inspiration, McKaelen Flynn, who is strong and wonderful and beautiful in so many ways. You are one-third of my heart and I love you.

313